Made of Rust and Glass

Volume III

OF RUST AND GLASS

Made of Rust and Glass, Volume III

Edited by Curtis A. Deeter, Leah McNaughton Lederman, and Jonie McIntire

Published by:
Of Rust and Glass
607 River Road
Maumee, OH 43537

Typesetting: Curtis A. Deeter

Cover Art: Sonny Lee EL

ISBN: 979-8-9877345-2-0

For Marshall Smith, beloved husband, father, poet, and friend. Rest well.

About the Cover Artist

Sonny Lee EL is an artist based in Columbus, Ohio. Born in Lima, Ohio and raised in South Florida, Sonny took influences from the Neon MTV Miami of the 80s and brought it back to the Rust Belt sensibility of the industrial Midwest. Working with canvas, paper, and digital media, he aims to use the language of color and shape to communicate in a world that seems constantly looking to the past while speeding furiously towards the future, somehow leaving the present undefined.

The artist on *9 to 5:*

"My goal with my work is to capture emotion and feeling that words cannot. As this piece came together, the posture and movement of the character reflected what it feels like going to work, day after day after day, like we all do. A sense of constant motion yet somehow not moving: a sensation I think we all feel in the air at the moment." –Sonny Lee EL

"Art is best derived from artless things."
–Jimmy Carter

Focus
by Dianne Borsenik

Dianne Borsenik is active in the northern and mid-Ohio poetry communities. Recent work appears in Slipstream, I Thought I Heard a Cardinal Sing: Ohio's Appalachian Voices *(Sheila-Na-Gig Editions, 2022), and* Pudding Magazine. *In 2019, Stubborn Mule Press published her full-length collection,* Raga for What Comes Next. *Lit Youngstown printed her poem "Disco" on their tee shirts, which makes her feel like a rock star. Find her on Facebook and at www.dianneborsenik.com.*

*—Elyria, Ohio, located
at the forks of the Black River,
23 miles southwest of Cleveland*

Elyria was a boom town back when
I was a kid. The county's factories
offered steady paychecks—with overtime—
to the Appalachian diaspora fleeing
the crushing poverty of the hills.
Entire families uprooted to resettle "up north,"
bringing brothers and uncles and cousins
with them to fill the floors of American Standard,
Ford Assembly, the US Steel plant.
All the stay-at-home mothers shopped
downtown, where Loomis' giant camera sign
flashed its giant lightbulb. We kids
were convinced it was taking our photos;
we always made faces at it.

Midway Mall killed the downtown in 1967—
and now it too stands dead and derelict.
All the major factories went bankrupt
or moved away, scraping the county
into the dustpan of the Rust Belt.
Cascade Park's sledding hill, where
generations of Elyrians picnicked
and watched fireworks every Fourth of July,
has been renovated into a broad road
sweeping down to a basin of spindly new trees.
Weeds fill the parking lots of restaurants;

empty buildings litter the strip malls.
The giant camera is long gone.

Black River, with its twin cascades, still
twists, tumbles, and flows through the heart
of Elyria, just as it did in 1817 when Heman Ely
founded the city. Loomis' giant camera sign
has turned up in a Cincinnati museum;
I'm sure kids still make faces at it. If only
it really had worked and captured the boom
before the bust. Before ghosted alleyways,
collapsed hopes, and the dissipation of *better*.
We kids who chose to stay—lucky enough
to have found jobs and kept homes—
now drive through Elyria's pot-holed,
siren-streaked streets, past the gap-toothed
grimace of downtown, picking our way
through the bones of a once-mighty behemoth.

Two Poems
by Tauno Ahonen

american loneliness

the man threw lye on the dead deer
i scanned the sky for turkey vultures
and other sky rats
such an undistinguished death
for such a majestic creature
its open eye full of infinite heartbreak
the closing of the last bookstore
true american loneliness

to my past lover

the ocean at sunrise
        is it a crime
           to stare

love you like cheap vodka
might not mean much to you
but for me it's almost too much
this one goes out to you
oh yeah and you

Dandy Joe's Last Buck Off
by Larry D. Sweazy

Larry D. Sweazy is the critically acclaimed, multiple-award-winning author of nineteen novels, one short story collection, and thirty-nine short stories, including the Trusty Dawson, U.S. Deputy Marshal Westerns, the Sonny Burton series, the Josiah Wolfe Westerns, and the Marjorie Trumaine Mysteries. A two-time Spur Award winner and recipient of the Western Fictioneers Peacemaker Award, he has also received four Will Rogers Medallion Awards. He's the winner of the Elmer Kelton Book Award, the Best Books of Indiana, and the Willa Award, and has been a Derringer Award finalist. Larry has worked as a freelance indexer for the last twenty-five years and teaches writing workshops across the country. He lives in Indiana with his wife, Rose, where he is hard at work on his next story. More information about Larry's work can be found on his website at larrydsweazy.com.

She wanted to tell Natalie to keep going. One more county over and they'd finally be out of Texas, free of everything it had ever done to them, to her, to the world. But she didn't say a word. It hurt too much to talk. Her fight with Texas would have to wait.

The pickup truck's headlights flashed on a shotgun-riddled green sign: Welcome to Hudspeth County. The dark road quickly returned, sliced by the twin high-beams. The starry sky went on forever, unconcerned with borders or time. Dawn was breaking behind them. The night said, "Come and get me," to the new day, with a defiant whisper of West Texas wind. It would lose and win. And win and lose. Not everybody was so lucky to get a second chance as light and darkness, duking it out over and over again. Natalie rolled the window down and tossed her cigarette out, unconcerned about the fire she might set. The ground was August-dry, brown as tweed and just as combustible.

Neither of them had said a word for the last hundred miles. A half bag of Funyons sat on the console. The Coke next to the rattling cellophane bag had lost its fizz. Maggie, Mags to Natalie, couldn't hear the words of the song on the radio; it was turned down too low. It wouldn't have mattered anyway. Country music sounded all the same, like stale convenience store cookies tasted. She wasn't in the mood for any good old boy music anyway. That would come soon enough.

The truck's tires whined against the road with the wobble of the front right forcing the rubber to dance with hardpan even though it didn't want to. Natalie had hit a fence post after too many Lone Stars after her last bull ride. Barbed wire had kissed the hood, got all tangled up in the grill like it had wanted to stay. Scars led the way everywhere they went.

Natalie rolled the window up three quarters of the way, allowing for the dry air to spin around inside the cab. The lights in the speedometer had burned out south of Dallas two years ago. She never knew how fast she was going. "At least it's not raining," she said, eyes on the road, then a quick sideways glance over to Mags.

Mags's tender face was pressed against the passenger window, cool, a relief to the flowery bruise on her cheek. The pain wasn't quite gone, but was distant, amassed with all of the other aches that screamed in a hallelujah chorus when she moved the wrong way. Her ribs were still wrapped, but she had ditched the ankle boot as soon as she could stand the pressure. Mobility, inertia, and flight were as important to her as breathing.

She let Natalie's words escape out of the window before she said anything. "He's gonna be there, you know."

"We have to eat. It's the only show in town."

"We're novelties, us girls riding bulls, like a freak show."

"You got something else you'd rather do other than worry too much about what other people think?"

"I got more than enough reason to worry. I can live on Funyons and Coke, thank you very much."

"I don't want to talk about it." This time it was Natalie's turn to shut down, not to talk. Her pain was scabbed over most days; blood running wild under the crust of her earthy skin, bubbling like lava. Mags could see what no one else could. Natalie didn't walk with a limp, but she carried a hollow spot in her heart that came out mean sometimes. They told them both that grief was unpredictable in counseling.

The truck pulled to the right, edged over to the rocky berm with a hard desire to take another tumble into a ditch. Mags watched Natalie fight the steering wheel, get serious again, focus on the road, then go for another Marlboro. Reds. The short ones. The original ones. Like her daddy smoked.

*****

The first time Mags sat on the back of an eighteen-hundred-pound bull, she could still feel whiskey burning on the back of her throat. This was BN (Before Natalie) when she was still living in Tilden, wide-eyed and nineteen without a crack in any of her bones. The bull, part Brahma, white and black with a slight hump behind his neck, had eyes that looked like they had been dipped in oil, and was called Lollipop. The bull had an easy reputation in the pen. The draw was a relief. But no bull likes a human, male or female, sitting on its back. Easy meant the beast was rideable for eight seconds a majority of time out the chute. Helmet and chaps on, her left hand was wrapped tight under the rope. She was surrounded by men. Her other hand was free. Had to be. That's how you drove a bull: one-handed. The flank man, Pete Grider, who had asked her to the homecoming dance in seventh grade, tested her one last time. "You sure you want to do this, Maggie?"

Her mouthpiece was in, protecting her teeth and shy smile, if that was possible. A kick to the jaw would shatter her life, her dreams. She'd seen that happen more than once; boys spitting out teeth, grown men crumbling to the ground into a fetal position, ambulances whirling away in the night taking the crowd's heart with it. She wasn't about to take the mouthpiece out any more than she was going to slow dance with Pete Grider. "Yup, I'm gonna do this," she'd mumbled.

Two bullfighters, both faces painted white with droopy fake smiles, stood in wait for the gate to be pulled: Hick and Jim from the local stable, runnin' buddies with rodeo dreams of their own. The gate puller, Toby Dorsey, rode bulls, too, had helped Mags train on the mechanical bucker that he'd built behind his garage. Then he'd let her ride his wild mare, Daisy, bareback. He'd given her the swig of Jack Daniel's before she'd made her way to the chute. Toby liked her, too, but was too bashful to say so. That was just as well.

Breathe in, breathe out. Lollipop bounced sideways against the rails, trying his best to pin her leg against the metal frame and shatter her kneecap. Mags could feel the heat of the bull rising up from underneath her. The smell of his anger was foul, like he'd ate a roadkill armadillo and puked it out. She'd wanted to ride a bull since she was twelve. Everybody told her she couldn't because she was a girl. That pissed her off. *Watch this.* She wore down every man and boy who told her no. *Teach me. Show me. What's that? How do you fall? Does it hurt? How do you get over the pain?* The boys in her family were called stocky. The girls were big boned. She was built for riding bulls if that mattered. It didn't matter to her. She would have done it anyway. It was like learning to fly. Live or die inside of eight seconds. She had to know what being alive felt like. Outside of the arena her life was forced, predictable, full of strife and secrets that everyone knew but her. She couldn't breathe at the dinner table. She couldn't do anything right inside the shadow of her house. Maybe if she learned to ride bulls, she would be free.

Mags leaned into the rail and made eye-contact with Toby. It would only take a second to back out, to be proud of herself for getting this far. If she quit now, she knew she'd never walk into another barn or see another rodeo for the rest of her life. That was something she couldn't imagine, life without the rodeo.

She leaned into the gate and nodded.

Toby pulled the gate and watched her every move.

Lollipop jumped at the chance to toss the human off his back. Four hooves in the air, a bend and thrust to the right, doing his best to find his own freedom; they were bound in the kinship of a heartbeat.

Mags rode for three seconds, never gained her center of balance, and flew off headfirst. She hit the ground hard. It echoed in the arena like a grandmother's slap to the face. Her lungs compressed, and she gasped for air; she felt like she was lost underwater. Her eyes rolled into the back of her head and her body twisted in the dirt until the two white-faced clowns taunted Lollipop away from her. The crowd groaned, all one hundred and fifty of them. Their disappointment encouraged her to her feet.

She dusted off her chaps, her mind still in those three seconds, trying to figure out where she went wrong. "I want to do it again," she said to Toby Dorsey as she passed by him, holding her head up as high as she could as she walked out off the floor, doing her best not to limp. *Give 'em a show. They'll ask you back.*

Lollipop didn't even offer her a parting glance.

Toby didn't ask her if she was sure this time. "Come by my place tomorrow. I can show you a thing or two about where you went wrong."

*****

Mags woke up first. Like usual, she was pushed into the corner of the truck cab, left to untangle herself from Natalie's soft places. They had always fit together like a broken beer bottle glued back together. Natalie was like twine, skinny, too fragile, you'd think to ride bulls, but she did. Her momma had entered her in a Texas-sized beauty pageant once when she was five, her blonde hair all piled up as high as it would go, curls bound in shiny new green velvet ribbons. She wore patent-leather shoes and an itchy crinoline under her dress. Natalie bit the judge when he asked her what she wanted to be when she grew up. "A horse," she'd said. She was like her daddy that way, too. She liked animals more than she liked people.

8

Sunlight beamed through the bug-splattered windshield and pain came back to life as Mags tried to move Natalie off her. It was the ribs first, then up her spine, to her face. She caught a glimpse of herself in the mirror. It could've been worse.

Natalie groaned and flashed her baby blues open; twinkling lights on an aluminum Christmas tree; Elvis's driveway at Graceland in December; the kind of eyes you can fall into and never find your way out of. Not every day was a holiday.

Mags smiled for a brief second. Movement caught her attention outside of the truck. "You better wake up, here comes Loretta."

Wide awake in an instant. "It's too early for Loretta. I gotta pee. Tell her to go away," Natalie said.

Tap, tap, tap. Knuckles on the window. "Hey, y'all. I didn't expect to see you here." Loretta Parker must have got up at four o'clock in the morning to do her hair, paint on her makeup, and slide into her skin-tight Wrangler's. Not a hair was out of place, and she looked like she'd walked straight out of a Shepler's catalog. She wore a bright red Stetson to match her lipstick, with shiny brunette hair flowing out from under the hat in waves. The ends of her hair curled up perfectly next to each other like an orderly paint-by-numbers picture of the sea. Her multiprint Bolero jacket was red, white, and blue, with little stars floating around it like she was the only planet in the universe. Her jeans were tucked into red cowboy boots that had never seen any kind of shit on the heels for longer than ten seconds. Loretta was married to Dip Parker, one of the top money earners on the circuit. They drove a shiny black Ford F-250 Dually and pulled an Airstream trailer everywhere they went. Mags was surprised fireworks didn't shoot out of the tailpipe.

Natalie piled out of the truck first, half-hunched over, eyed a pink Port-A-Potty, and garbled, "Good morning, Loretta," as she hurried by her.

Mags followed, easing onto the ground as gently as she could, fighting off the urge to stretch.

"Oh, honey," Loretta said, ignoring Natalie, focusing her full gaze on Mags, "I heard you took a tough fall in Waco, but I didn't know it was this bad. You should be home in bed instead of traipsin' around half of Texas tryin' to keep up with Natalie." Loretta turned to the pink toilet just as the door closed. "She knows he's gonna be here, doesn't she?" It was a low whisper; gossip; a secret shared on the sly.

Mags wanted a tall coffee and six ibuprofens. She didn't want to be standing in the middle of a field talking to Loretta Parker. She never wanted to talk to Loretta. "She knows. I think that's why we're here. She hasn't said so. Doesn't need to, I guess."

The sky was as blue as the dusty China in her hope chest and blank of any clouds. Pickup trucks, horse trailers, and a variety of campers sat parked in a semi-circle in front of the rickety white barn that held the arena. Somebody was frying bacon.

"Do you need anything, honey?" Loretta said.

"Coffee and a winning lottery ticket would be nice. I hear Tahiti is nice this time of year."

"That's over by Fort Worth, isn't it? I've never been there. Maybe Dip'll take me, you think?"

Mags restrained herself. It would hurt too much to do anything else. "You should ask him."

Loretta smiled. Piano keys so white they hurt your eyes. "You stay right there. I'll get you and Natalie a coffee. Cream and sugar?"

"You don't have a fresh Coke, do you?"

"I thought you said you wanted coffee."

"That's for Natalie. I never touch the stuff."

"Dip won't let me buy nothin' but Dr. Pepper. That all right?"

"No, thanks."

Loretta stalked off toward the Airstream on a mission. Mags stood there, letting the sun warm her face, trying not to move the wrong way and set off another spasm of pain. She closed her eyes and took a deep breath. Her mind didn't have far to wander. It always went back to Waco. She'd got cocky, sat too loose, didn't respect the bull. She stopped time in the middle of a somersault and wondered if she could change the outcome. It was a short wonder. She knew the answer. The past couldn't be changed.

Natalie's boots hit the ground as she fled the giant pink bubblegum shithole, forcing Mags back to the present.

"How'd you get rid of the Trophy?" Natalie said.

"Do you really have to call her that?"

"It's the truth."

"You don't like it when someone calls you a name that's true."

Natalie stared at Mags, her hair still a nest of cowlicks. "You need a Coke."

"All she had was Dr. Pepper."

"Figures."

Mags was about to say something to change the subject, like, *"Let's find the showers,"* but the words got caught in her throat and never came out. Instead, she watched a beat-up green Chevy Silverado towing a creaky livestock trailer turn off the road.

10

Natalie followed her stare. "Shit, he really *is* gonna be here."

Mags didn't say anything. Cottonmouth came on quick. She forgot all of her pain and felt Natalie's broken heart all over again. "We can leave," she was finally able to say.

"We were gonna cross paths sooner or later. I'd just as soon get this over. If we leave now, I'll never come back."

Mags nodded, knew what she meant—*no more rodeos*—and kept her eyes on the trailer. They both stood silent, didn't even notice as Loretta joined them. She stood next to Natalie, holding a steaming cup of strong coffee and a Dr. Pepper, her mouth slightly agape.

Bobby Hutchens parked the trailer with precision, got out, dusted his black cowboy hat off, put it on, then loped around to the back of the trailer. He was tall as a sunflower, skinny as the stalk, his head and hat just a bit oversized for his body. They all watched as Bobby unloaded Dandy Joe, a two-thousand-pound bull, silently, like they were at the start of a party forbidden to do anything but mourn.

*****

Natalie and Mags were there that night. They both wished they hadn't been but were glad they had been in the end. It was one of those weird intersections of life that felt like fate two days later. Neither of them had rode in that show. They were spectators, princesses in the court of Billy Charles.

Some of the men who did what Billy did refused to be called a rodeo clown, opting instead for the more honest title of bullfighter, but Billy didn't mind being a clown. The crowd expected a clown and that's what they got, a prat fall, a laugh, a performance. He was short and skinny like Natalie, his only child, his hair blond like hers at one time, too. He was bald as a hundred-thousand-mile tire and had grown a little pouchy belly. His body was hidden in the oversized clothes that he wore, that all of the clowns wore. No restraint. They had to move free and fast. Billy had always looked a lot bigger than he really was.

They sat in the stands, surrounded by friends and rarely seen rodeo family. Billy had taken Natalie with him everywhere when she was a kid. She'd grown up in an arena and on the road. One day there was three of them, then her momma ran off with a fella who made the winner's belt buckles, never to be seen or heard from again. The next day, it was just the two of them warming up pork and beans for dinner, wrapping sprained ankles in a drafty camper. Natalie looked for her mother every time her boot sole hit rodeo dirt, but she never saw her again.

That night, Billy outdanced bull after bull, doing flips and sways, showing off for Natalie, all the while capturing the crowd's heart. Billy, of course, hadn't always been a clown. He was a junior championship calf roper by the time he was six, then moved on to bucking broncs, and finally riding bulls. His collection of belt buckles could cover a two-story wall, but he kept them in a storage unit outside of San Antonio. After he broke his arm for the third time, he took up bullfighting and had been doing it ever since. He figured as long as he could run and laugh, he could keep chasing the rodeo rainbow.

It was the middle of the show when Dandy Joe jumped out of the chute, joining the dance, just another eight second ride for Raul Astova. But Raul's hand got stuck in the wrap after the horn sounded, and Billy rushed in too close, distracted by something in the stands. Dandy Joe did nothing with intent, nothing any other bull wouldn't do. He wasn't a murderous bull. He was trying to survive the moment in his own way just like everyone else. He swung to left and his sawed-off horn slammed into the side of Billy's head, sending him flying. Clowns don't wear helmets.

Raul managed to free his hand and tumbled out of Dandy Joe's reach, but Billy never got up again. He lingered for two days, tubes running in and out of his broken body, machines beeping, lights flashing. Natalie had to tell them to pull the plug.

*****

There wasn't a line at the registration table. Mags hung back as Natalie paid her entry fee and pulled her draw out of the box. *Please don't let it be him.* It wasn't. Natalie drew Hostage Taker, a black three-year-old bull who weighed in at a little over fifteen hundred pounds. The bull had twenty-two attempts and fifteen rides. Natalie had a chance. It was a good draw. Mags relaxed as they headed over to the pen to check Hostage Taker out.

Glenn Carrigan owned Hostage Taker and hailed from Blanco County. He was new to the circuit, so nobody knew much about him or his bulls. The numbers did the talking.

They stopped at the pen. Natalie climbed up on the first metal rung to get a better look.

"I'm glad you didn't draw Dandy Joe," Mags said.

Natalie didn't turn around, talked straight ahead, focused on Hostage Taker. "He rides right before me."

"That was close."

"I would have ridden him. Given him a good gouge or a kick to the head if I could have."

"I wouldn't have watched."

"Yes, you would have." Natalie popped off the fence, smiled wider than she had since they'd pulled in. "That bull is money."

"I hope so." Mags restrained her own smile. She'd save that for later, when Natalie was back on the ground, standing on two feet.

*****

They passed the time in the truck, avoiding Loretta, Dandy Joe, and most everyone else. Natalie was quieter than usual on ride days. Mags missed the anticipation of the arena. Her chance to sit on a bull was months away. This layoff was long, painful, and unplanned. If Natalie didn't string together some wins, they'd both be standing behind the cash register at the Seven-Eleven sooner rather than later.

Mags was in the stands, sitting by herself. Natalie was in the long hall that led to the chute with her chest protector and chaps on, ready to ride. A helmet dangled from her fingers. They both watched Dandy Joe's every move as he pushed into the gate. Once the bull was settled, Dip Parker eased onto Dandy Joe's back. Dip wore a flawless black Stetson hat and a sponsor's vest that didn't show any daylight between patches. Loretta was sitting three rows off the arena floor. She'd already waved Mags down three times. Mags shook her head each time. She wanted to see this one on her own, be as close to the rafters as she could get. If anybody could ride Dandy Joe, it was Dip Parker.

The gate puller swung the gate open, and Dandy Joe jumped out of the pen with Dip's left hand in the air. Dip leaned back as far as he could go, perfectly balanced, as the bull did everything he could to toss the man off him. Nothing worked. It was like Dip Parker had Super-Glued himself to the bull. Dandy Joe twisted, turned, and bucked, but eight seconds later, Dip was still riding. The horn sounded and the crowd erupted into a chorus of victorious cheers. Loretta was on her feet jumping up and down like the cheerleader she was. Dip slipped off the bull and landed on his feet. He ran to the fence, jumped up, and waved his hat to everyone in the arena. The gladiator was home.

Two bullfighters, dressed like usual in loose clothes, both wearing greasepaint, did their best to corral Dandy Joe, but he'd stopped in the middle of the arena and refused to be moved. He stood statue-still, eyeing the celebrating Dip, ignoring the clowns. Drool fell to the floor from the bull's swollen lips. Mags was relieved but couldn't take her eyes off of Dandy Joe. Natalie was already readying herself to climb onto Hostage Taker. The show was over.

One of the bullfighters pushed Dandy Joe from the side, drawing his attention for a second. The bull flicked its tail, then bolted straight for Dip, who was still waving to the crowd. But Dip was aware of everything around him. A man like him didn't collect as many winner's buckles as he had by being a fool. He saw Dandy Joe charging at him and jumped the rest of the way over the fence.

Dandy Joe didn't slow down. He didn't stop.

Mags was on her feet when the bull ran headfirst into the gate post. It sounded like a freight train had crashed through the building. The sound of the hit echoed upward, then exploded outward. Every inch of the bull's body shimmied as it bounced backward, whiplashed and dazed. He fell to the ground with another loud thud, then groaned and spit blood from his mouth. He kicked his legs but couldn't get any traction. The arena fell silent. Mags had seen some enraged bulls do strange things before, but nothing like this.

Two seconds later, Dandy Joe started to convulse and wail. Then just as fast, he shut down. Quit moving, except a heavy pant, exhaling pain as quick as he could. The clowns cleared the way for Bobby Hutchens and the vet, an old gent in a white coat, that probably had a local practice up the street, to get to the bull. Dandy Joe didn't have it in him to fight them off. He snorted and moaned. His riding days were over. The vet had no choice but to go for the needle and put Dandy Joe down.

Natalie had climbed off Hostage Taker and made her way to the middle of the arena. Tears flowed from her eyes. Mags couldn't get to her, couldn't push her way through the crowd. They were a concrete wall shielding her from the worst kind of death. Mags would have pulled the trigger if she'd had a gun.

*****

Natalie sat in the driver's seat, with the window rolled down. Dip and Loretta were standing next to the truck, hand in hand, the sun setting behind them. "We'll see you in Fort Worth in a few days. You gonna be all right, aren't you, Honey?" Loretta said to Natalie. Mags was stuffed in the passenger seat with a fresh Coke in her hand.

"We wouldn't miss it," Natalie said. She dropped the truck into drive and held her foot on the brake. "Thanks for everything."

Dip and Natalie nodded as she pulled away. "You drive careful now," Dip hollered out. The morning sun gleamed off his new winner's belt buckle.

Natalie nodded and drove to the edge of the field. She stopped at the road and looked to Mags. "How about I turn left instead of right?"

"What's in New Mexico?"

"I don't know," Natalie said. "Maybe it's time to find out."

Mags nodded and fished out a stale Funyon from the bag in the

14

console. "I think you're right. We'll have to get jobs."

"We'll find us a barn somewhere. I don't mind shoveling shit until you heal. We'll be all right."

Mags smiled, even though it still hurt. "I think we will be."

Natalie did turn left instead of right, but she hit the brakes. The truck pulled against her, but she fought it back, and they came to a stop. "No. If we go west, we'll never come back. I want to ride here, at home, in Texas. I don't know any place else, and neither do you. We won't have to worry about running across Dandy Joe ever again. You'll be better soon, then we'll be in the money for sure. I'm tired of tryin' to outrun ghosts or coming face to face with them. We got buckles of our own to win."

"So, we're going to Fort Worth?"

"Looks that way."

Mag didn't say anything else. She popped open a fresh Coke to wash down the stale Funyons and settled in for the ride.

Along the Shores of Lake Charlevoix

by Miranda Keskes

Miranda Keskes is a writer and educator whose fiction appears in Blink Ink, Pigeon Review, Does It Have Pockets, 50-Word Stories, Every Day Fiction, The Drabble, *and elsewhere. Her work has been nominated for Best Microfiction and Best Small Fictions. She lives in Michigan with her husband and their two boys. She writes the Substack publication,* The Teachers' Lounge. *You can find her on Instagram at miranda_keskes_writer.*

I was catching tadpoles when I saw a mermaid. I was a boy—just five years old. We were camping at Young State Park, our annual summer vacation spot. I spent hours exploring the park's sandy shoreline, the waves of Lake Charlevoix lapping along its edge. Small pools of water scattered along the beach's eastern edge. Every year, the frogs spawned and the pools teemed with tadpoles.

I scooped them up into my cupped hands. They zigged and zagged, their tails tickling my palms. Out of the corner of my eye, I saw a flash of red hair and green flippers bobbing in and out of the waves of the lake.

Mesmerized, I watched as this sea nymph emerged from the water, removed her flippers and mask and walked onto the beach. As she approached, I realized she wasn't much older than me.

"Catchin' tadpoles?" she asked.

I nodded.

"Can I help?"

I nodded again.

We spent the rest of the afternoon by those pools. I kept looking at her feet, waiting for them to sprout into a tail.

*****

We met on the beach every summer after that. My family and I were recurring tourists. She was a local who lived in a small cottage on the outskirts of Boyne City. She always came to find me. We filled our summer days riding bikes along the park's wooded trails, fishing for perch and walleye off the docks in town, and hunting for Petoskey stones along the shoreline, but our favorite pastime was catching tadpoles.

16

She was twelve when she told me she once believed tadpoles turned into mermaids. "Isn't that silly?" she said. Our heads were close. The summer breeze tugged at a strand of her red hair. It tickled my face.

I shook my head. She smiled, then ran to the water's edge and dove in. I raced after her.

*****

When I was nineteen, we arrived at the shoreline by water. With a portion of my savings, I bought an old aluminum fishing boat. "More like a dinghy," she said with a laugh, before leaning in to kiss me.

Once we were shallow enough, I dropped an anchor and waded the rest of the way in while she seemed to glide. I patted the zipped pocket of my swim shorts, where the majority of my savings had gone.

We walked along the beach holding hands, heading towards the small pools along the eastern edge. As soon as we arrived, we laughed and dove after the darting tadpoles.

We were covered in muddy sand as the sun began to set. She winked, then ran towards the water and shallow-dived in. She was an agile swimmer. It wasn't long before I could see only flashes of red hair and the green of her swimsuit shimmering in the distance.

When she returned, emerging from the lake, I was down on one knee. She nodded, tears in her eyes. I took her face and cupped it with the palms of my hands.

*****

For sixty more years, we returned to these shallow pools along the beach. This is the first time I return without her.

It's early in the season. Instead of tadpoles, my granddaughter and I see jelly-like globs floating in the water: frog eggs.

She tugs on my hand. "Look!" She points and we bend down together to watch as several tadpoles wriggle within the eggs. One breaks free and begins to swim. My granddaughter laughs, clapping.

"Grandpa, is it true that tadpoles turn into mermaids?"

"What do you think?"

"That's what Grandma used to say."

I smile. "Then it must be true." My gaze drifts to the waves in the distance, looking for a flash of red hair.

Poem for my BFF, DZ

by Sam Wright

Sam Wright is an award-winning poet, environmental activist, and a retired English teacher. His poetry and cover photos have appeared in the last three issues of Best of Ohio. His work has also appeared in Peace and Planet News, Common Threads, A Rustling and Waking Within, Encore, The [Toledo] City Paper, Of Rust and Glass, *and others. A lifelong Toledoan, he and his wife recently pulled up stakes and moved to Lakewood, Ohio to better enjoy their grandkids.*

We have been best of friends for better than fifty years,
since the Jesuits had a go at us in high school.

I write to you now from my tent pitched on a remote shoreline
opposite yours. Even from a distance, I recognize you perfectly.

I regret, as you do, that over the years our convictions
have drawn us to opposing camps, my left, your right.

We have debated the existence of god and hell, a woman's
right to choose, the growing acceptance of homosexuality.

You pray for me and wonder where I went wrong.
I scratch my head and wonder what miscalculations led you astray.

Our convictions have sharpened our tongues, dulled our
hearing, hardened our thinking, but friends we remain.

Like an old married couple, we haven't lost the ability to
Complete each other's sentences.
That's an intimacy not easily discarded.

So be generous when, during challenging times, I tell you
I do not hunger for your prayers—that good juju works fine for me.

And when I row my boat across the divide, white flag flying,
know that rather than risk the damage of reckless debate

I have come to ask you to join me for a quiet afternoon of
fishing subject only to the whims of wind and worm.

You may assume the helm as together we drift
mere inches above the inscrutable depths below

two friends on a common cosmic journey, sharing worms,
a wet towel to clean our hands before a snack, and

an occasional remark on the beauty of the day.
It is those small things that bind my soul to yours, my friend.

While you long to be a fisher of men, share with me
this day's blessing upon both our camps. That is enough for me.

Ode to Forty-Five
by David James

David James has published seven books; his most recent is Alive in Your Skin While You Still Own It, *2022. More than thirty of his one-act plays have been produced in the U.S. and Ireland.*

nothing you say or do
matters to me anymore

I don't care what kind of toilet you shit on or off
I care less about what you sign or where you go

I wake up and smile with no fist of despair in the core
      of my stomach/no squealing in my ears
      about what I might hear on the radio or TV
      about a tweet/a curse/more name-calling

god/my nerves are lying back on lounge chairs
falling asleep under a big willow tree

my nerves are singing along to John Denver songs/
making guacamole
with bacon and lime/it's been years since I felt this good

I feel like I'm standing in the world hall of fame/
amazed to find out that/hell/
      I'm one of the inductees

One potato, two potato…
by Chad Broughman

Chad V. Broughman was the recipient of the Rusty Scythe Prize Book award and the Adobe Cottage Writers Retreat honor. Chad has published two short story collections— the forsaken *and* slighted—*and is anthologized in* On Loss, Scribes Valley, *and* Write Michigan. *His fiction is in journals worldwide, including* Carrier Pigeon, River Poets Journal, Sky Island Journal, Pulp Literature, *and* From Whispers to Roars, *and he is a Best of the Net and Pushcart Prize nominee. Chad teaches English and Creative Writing at the secondary/post-secondary levels but is most proud of his role as father of two rambunctious young sons.*

As the waiter lays down the oblong plate, Eva's heart thuds in her mouth. A glance across the table, her husband-to-be nods. She centers on the sweet potato, orange flesh vivid atop the white ceramic. And her eyes ice over. Big city lights stream through the restaurant's windows, so manufactured compared to the starshine of her northern Michigan youth.

"You certain I can't offer you an entrée, ma'am? A side-dish?" Eva shakes her head, still fixed on the potato's rose-colored skin, tapered at the ends. One hand wields her fork like a warrior; with the other, she beckons her fiancé in a come-hither motion, manages to feign a rigid, half-smile deep in her jowls.

Her beloved lifts the ramekin high. "Don't understand this, darling"—he pours brown sugar atop the spud, evenly, as if he's practiced many times—"But I'm all ears when you're ready." The rich scent wafts outward, transporting Eva to her childhood table.

*****

The Murray house smells of smoked meat. Eva watches her ten-year-old self stirring the black-eyed peas, pigtails pulled tight. Pa plops into his chair, suspenders hanging like lassos. Besides the slosh of Ma doling out vittles, it's quiet. Eva ogles the sugar bowl, glistening in the burn of the kerosene lamp. Sugar is a rarity, especially since Pa's talk about unions and slumping demand for iron-ore. All Eva knows is that he only goes to the mine twice a week now. And that her breaths are shorter, like she's always running.

After grace, Eva dives into the tuber, heaping the cinnamon and sweetener high as a sand dune. She rubs her hands together, waits. Ma smiles at her indulgence. With real ones, her upper teeth show, the folds by her eyes soften. With nervous ones, her lower jaw sets, neck muscles clench like a bat's wing. And with pretend ones, Pa is always nearby.

Right away, Eva knows her mistake. Her stomach doubles up. She wants to scoop it all back, quick as she can. But it's best to sit still, take what's coming. Pa clears his throat, studies the speckled mound in front of her. After filling their tins with water, Ma starts sputtering, trying to fix things. "Kids never understand money troubles. Only know when something tastes good."

Pa drains his cup, dips his head for Ma to refill it, but he raises his arm too fast. Eva flinches, reaching for the back of her scalp where he'd once jerked her braids for nibbling on some pone before prayers. Strange to see her own butter-yellow hair tangled in his fat fingers, drooping like corn silk.

"There's a picnic at St. Michaels after mass," Ma drivels on. With every word, Eva feels sicker. "Maybe Deacon Johnson'll play his fiddle. We'll make applesauce to pass, I s'ppose—"

Pa eyes Ma until she falls silent then stuffs a jumble of pheasant and beans into his mouth. After some time, Ma tests the waters and starts eating, too. Eva follows suit, taking in dollops of stew, hoping to appear soft-pedalled while stealing glimpses of the menacing pile she made. Between bites, she flattens the sugar with the bowl of her spoon, pressing into the potato's core. She sees Ma eating like a bird, and vows to herself—never fake smile like Ma does.

Yet the storm doesn't come. Eva is dismissed to wash dishes, head for bed. Afraid to eat the potato, she dumps it in the trash, brushes scraps over top. In her cot, she keeps an eye open, praying it's not too good to be true, that Pa really is too tuckered to fight.

*****

Making her way to breakfast the next morning, Eva sees Pa sipping coffee, peering over his tin. The unease is touchable. Ma is already prattling away. Sliding out her chair, Eva looks down at the fried eggs and hash. Atop them, a grainy drift of brown sugar, four fingers high. Sugar bowl sits empty. "Heard there's a loose heifer in the town-square," Ma sputters. Eva's lungs pull like rubber. As she stares at the clotted mess, her eyes dampen. For a fleeting moment, she hates both parents evenly.

"We got plenty of money, ain't we, girl?" Pa says. Then he slurps some coffee. "Hell, we'll buy all the goddamn sugar in Michigan." Aiming a stumpy finger, he commands, "Go on, child. Waste not, want not."

Belly stirring, Eva digs to the bottom of the mishmash, scrapes her spoon against the plate, metal on metal. The shredded potatoes are caked with broken yolks that drip down her chin as she shovels in the wreckage. When the thickness overwhelms her, she pushes the gritty mix into her cheeks like a rodent. After the urge to retch passes, she gulps the syrupy bolus and scoops up more, holding Pa's gaze until he rises, then steps outside, cup in hand. By the wash basin, Ma stands mute. Her silence throbbing like a wound.

In the privy, Eva throws up. She wipes her mouth with the back of her hand, looks across the sloping field to the Lovett farm below, praying to catch a peek of them doing simple things, family things––kids rolling hoops; their Pa shoeing a colt; or Mrs. Lovett hanging blankets on the line. Anything at all.

*****

There's a stranger among them, just Eva, her groom-to-be, and the steaming sweet potato. She swallows the swell in her throat, announces with resolve, "I'm pregnant"––a quick peek upward––"And I'll love fiercely, you and this child"––then glowers at the plate again. The muscles in her face begin to pull, forging into that old, familiar sham. But she sucks in hard, spreads a thumb and fingers across her stretching cheeks. And like a fox gone rabid, she strokes. Over and over, until the skin goes slack. "But in this moment, I'm plugging up some things." All pretense faded from her lips, Eva rears the fork overhead. "It's finished," she says. And like a vigilante set afire, stabs downward.

Sweat From Our Foreheads
by Dan Denton

Dan Denton is a former union autoworker turned full time writer. His poetry and short stories are widely published, and he is the author of multiple novels including his most recent The Dead and the Desperate *(Roadside Press, 2023).*

we wipe sweat from our foreheads
as giant industrial fans
hum above us
fans made impotent
by heat
and humidity

bosses breathe down our necks
as we hang precariously
to middle class life
one step ahead of the repo man

we wipe sweat from our foreheads
while the CEO collects luxury sports cars
mansions
and civic awards

investors hoard dividends
and build small fortunes
dividends earned by our carpal tunnel
and varicose veins
fortunes built by our arthritis
and surgically repaired backs

we wipe sweat from our foreheads
waiting to hear if our name
is on the Sunday overtime list
we don't ask for anything
but a chance to feed our families
we don't ask for anything
but health insurance
and a chance to retire
while we can still walk

we wipe sweat from our foreheads
while limping out of the gates
we crawl into our Jeeps
and drive home to working class neighborhoods
we eat dinner
and collapse into recliners
to watch sports
on our big screen TVs

we swallow down some aspirin
and fall asleep in our beds
and sleep about half of the recommended hours needed
to live a healthy life

we wipe sweat from our foreheads
and watch our dreams
slip away into the night

we wipe sweat from our foreheads
while worrying about paying for braces
or for our daughter's college tuition

we wipe sweat from our foreheads
while never asking for a goddamn thing
but a chance to push our kids
a little higher up the caste system

we're a proud bunch
us factory rats
we sweat and we bleed
we ache and we limp

we wipe sweat from our foreheads
while politicians talk about us
like we're numbers on a chart

we wipe sweat from our foreheads
and we barely notice
the industrial fans
that hum above us

How Quickly We Become Skeletons

by Alex Weilhammer

Alex Weilhammer grew up in a suburb of Indianapolis, graduated from DePauw University, and earned my MFA from The New School. His work has appeared in Stat(o)rec, Spiritus Mundi Review, Teachers & Writers Magazine, the Sarasota Herald-Tribune, *and the* Indianapolis-Star. *He is an English teacher in Indianapolis, where he lives with his wife, cat, and dog.*

I

Robert Acton is driving toward sunset in his red GMC Terrain. Already the new commute between Indianapolis and Cloverdale feels routine: flat farmland; smatterings of trees and shrubs; the occasional barn or truck stop gas station. Each way takes 50 minutes. At least he still enjoys the new car smell. At least he feels tall as he looks down on the much-diminished Sedan driving some three seconds in front of him as they both cruise down the right lane.

He squints against the sun while gripping the steering wheel with both hands. The Sedan's body paint is a withering gray, and the driver is smoking a nearly finished cigarette. He considers the Sedan's dry, itchy upholstery, its faded blue likely reeking of tobacco. As bad as this Sedan looks, it's not nearly as bad as the Plymouth Reliant he rode around in as a child. Mom and Dad both smoked in that car, sometimes simultaneously. Shortly after turning 11, he realized asking them to stop only made it worse.

The woman driving the Sedan dangles the smoldering ember out of her window, wrist poised in nonchalance. The cigarette falls and bounces hard on the pavement, bounces *high.* Robert blinks once and it's gone. He blinks again then checks his left-side mirror. The cigarette careens into the left lane, tumbling over itself in erratic gyrations. The ember glows a tenacious orange that refuses to die.

In his side mirror, Robert spots a sports car in the left lane. It's maybe ten seconds back but gaining quickly on the Terrain. Robert checks the Sedan then squints back into his rearview, letting off the gas pedal so he can study his soon-to-be passer.

The Camaro boasts a metallic-Transformer-shade of orange that nearly dissolves into the blurring, ochre farmland. Robert wishes he was the one driving that car. Instead of driving to his apartment, he'd go south down 231 toward his parents' house. He'd weave through traffic like an ice skater, and Pink Floyd would be blasting out of his rolled down windows. After going past the Wal-Mart, he'd be nearly there—just a hop, skip, and a jump. Once he pulled up to their house, he'd lay on the horn for as long as it took. He wouldn't care if the whole street came out to yell at him. He'd lay on that horn until they stumbled outside their house, and once they saw it was him in there, he'd hock a loogie out of the passenger window right into their "yard." Then, before peeling out, he'd rev the engine into a frenzy so loud it screamed I-fucking-told-you-so.

He can't pull off a stunt like that now. The Terrain—it's nice, sure—but it lacks the flare of the Camaro that's still inching closer. Plus, Allie would never let him get away with it. He hears her now: "What, you think you're some cool guy, with that little Camaro of yours? You think it's still gonna be cool when you're still paying for that thing 60 years from now?" No, she'd never let him buy such a vehicle in the first place; she'd suggest a safe, family car, like a GMC Terrain. She'd remind him about the child they'd soon be having before making up some aphorism like, "Babies and sports cars, they just don't mix."

The Sedan's brake lights flare up, snapping Robert out of his stupor. After tapping on his own brakes, he's annoyed. His irritation is quickly replaced, however, by the odd sensation of realizing he zoned out on the road. How many trees has he passed since noticing the Camaro? Robert checks his left side mirror and sees the Transformer is about to pass his Terrain.

The Sedan pops a tire—veers sharp into the left lane. The Terrain *just* misses the Sedan's right-side bumper—crosses the shoulder—skirts along the grass. There's a deafening smack—a thick crunch. A sound so loud it slows down time. Despite closing his eyes, Robert perfectly imagines the Camaro's grill smashing right into the Sedan's driver-side door.

Did she fucking die? Robert asks himself. He squirms against the tightness of his seatbelt. He feels sweat on his forehead and temples, and a terrible chill reaper-dances down his spine. He thinks to check his rearview but immediately decides against it. He doesn't want to know, doesn't have to know, wasn't involved. He presses on the gas pedal, slightly reassured by the sound of the Terrain's surging power, by the energy taking him further and further away from whatever lurks behind.

*****

27

"Yeah, I'm sorry, Allie, but I can't tonight." His butt crashes into the recliner in their living room. His eyes snap shut, and he drapes the back of his hand on his forehead. "I've got this terrible headache."

"Sorry to hear that," he hears her say behind him, probably from their bedroom. He imagines her tidying the pillows or adjusting the plants on the windowsill. He takes deep breaths through his nose and sinks backward, hoping to glean as much relief as he can from the recliner's plushness. He hears steps behind him, the sound growing louder. "Rough day at work, or what?"

"You know," he replies before releasing another large exhale, "work was fine, but on the drive home, I got this headache out of nowhere." It's not a lie exactly, he thinks. He does have a headache, a slight one at least. Can guilt cause headaches? "I feel bad cause I know we've been talking about this Target trip."

"Yeah, yeah, it's all good, Robert." Her tone dips, indicative of reluctant acceptance. His guilt-ache sharpens. "I'm not getting all that much, anyway. Here."

He feels a warm rag drape across his forehead. He opens his eyes. She stands there with a sweet half-smile, arm outstretched as she adjusts the rag. Her curly, sandy-blonde hair is once again in a ponytail, and she's wearing an old pair of his sweatpants and a wrinkled V-neck. Outside of the seven-month bulge in her belly, she looks the same as she always does after a double management shift at Waffle House. He notes a radiant glow that starts from the back of her eyes.

"Thanks, hon. I don't deserve you."

"Mhm," she replies, now donning a three-quarter smile. "I'll get you some ibuprofen and water, too."

He sinks in deeper to the recliner and flattens the warm rag against his skin. He remembers one night, he was about seven, when his Mom yelled at his Dad for parking in the grass again. "Do you not know how to fucking drive or something? How many times I got to tell you? You're gonna kill that grass, you keep parking like that!"

"Will you just shut the fuck up," his Dad yelled from the kitchen, "or are you gonna bitch like this all night?"

A screaming match ensued. After what felt like a half an hour, Robert had had enough. He stomped out into the living room, screamed as loud as he could: "*Stop fighting, stop it!*" But on the last "stop," his voice cracked like an egg. Mom and Dad decided to redirect their anger to him. "Mind your fucking business!" "Don't you *dare* scream at us!" "This don't concern you, kid!"

"Here ya go," Allie says. When did she even run the sink? He takes the glass and two pills with a nod. He hears the crash again and again and again. The sound is a combination of a smack and a twist, or maybe a rip and a screech. Almost a moan.

"Thanks, Allie. Again, I'm sorry I can't make this trip with you."

"It's okay, really. But since I'm the one buying and hauling this crib back home, you're gonna be the one to build it! I'll tell you that right now!" She's amused. He can tell because of her pushiness, which is her way of being endearing. The amount of Yelp reviewers she's created on assertive charm alone should be enough for some kind of award. He imagines her at work as he looks into her glowing eyes: "Now, you're gonna write us a good review, right? Gonna tell *everyone* on Yelp how yummy those eggs were, how crispy the home fries were, all that good stuff, right?" She is a master of the imperative question, and that meant he'd be building that crib before the week was out.

"Yes, I am. I will." He swallows the pills. "Listen, I was thinking. Do you remember our friend Jayson? The guy who runs that AutoZone down in Beech Grove?"

"Sure. Why?"

"Well, I just remembered when he let us joy ride those sports cars. You remember that?"

"Oh, yeah, sure. I recall going way faster than you ever did."

"Shit, I mean, yeah. You were the one trying to get up to 120; I just wanted to rev the engines."

"I have a need for speed, what can I say. What makes you bring that up?"

"I saw this Camaro today, is all. It was a beauty."

"What, you want one now? I know you got that nice new coding job, honey, but I don't think we're making Camaro money anytime soon. Plus, with the baby? I don't see that working out too well."

He couldn't help but to smile.

"No, no, I don't want one. Seeing it just reminded me of that time. I like our Terrain."

"Speaking of which, you got the keys?"

"Oh. Right. Here you go."

"What's wrong?"

"What do you mean?"

"I don't know. There's something going on in your eyes. Like you're thinking about something else."

"Oh, yeah, sorry. Just this headache has my mind trailing off."

"Positive?"

"Yes, honey. I am. Thanks for all of this, seriously."

"Yeah, yeah, yeah. You'd do the same for me. I'm gonna head out. See ya in a bit."

"All right, hon." He gulps as he watches her walk away. A jolt rattles his chest. "Um—uh—"

She turns around, one foot in the kitchen, the other still planted in their living room, her radiant eyes expectant. He imagines Allie's head smashing on the steering wheel as the Terrain lifts into the air from a terrible collision. He watches it play out in his mind's eye in slow motion. Their child rotating abruptly, breaking its newly formed bones, bleeding—

"Be safe out there, all right?"

II

Three weeks later, Robert is on his way to work, driving nearly 10 miles below the speed limit in the right lane. It's a dreary day, but the Terrain's windshield wipers are making easy work of the rain. Robert doesn't appreciate this fact, however. Instead, he's worrying about whether something might be wrong with his tires. He thought he felt something amiss after driving over a pothole the other day. Maybe the dealership failed to properly check the vehicle before putting it on the market. It could happen. Robert makes a mental note to look up whether something like that has happened before, a faulty screw popping off a tire five weeks after purchase.

A white Honda Accord trails behind the Terrain, a little too close for comfort. Its plain color washes into the overcast sky. A semi, also white but grayed with time, drives ahead of the Terrain. Robert makes out a Target logo on the back of its cargo. He considers the nearing headlights in his rearview, but after reconsidering the semi, he lets off the gas to decelerate, hoping the driver behind him will get the message.

He blinks through the bleariness in his eyes and tightens his grip on the steering wheel. Once again, he feels like he didn't get enough sleep last night. He has been sweating in bed as well, much to Allie's annoyance. He hates disturbing her not because he's scared of her reaction but because she doesn't deserve it. He knows how stir-crazy she's been not while not working. To heap his tossing and turning, his nightly headaches, and his bed-sweating onto her boredom feels akin to betrayal. Perhaps his body is crying out to Allie, anxious to tell her the truth about the crash he abandoned for fear of being responsible, for fear of what he'd see. But it's almost been a month now. It's too late to tell her, right? He hopes he can let it fade like the exhaust fumes spewing from the semi ahead. What if, after work, he visits the job site in Brownsburg where their new house is being built? He could take some photos, chat with the laborers, and visualize the ideal spot for a swing set. That would be a nice update for Allie; maybe that would indicate his commitment to this huge transition in their life, would counterbalance his evening aloofness.

As the Accord maintains its closeness, Robert notes a bad feeling brewing in his gut. If it isn't the tires, maybe something is wrong with the engine. He turns off the radio and listens for unknown sounds. What if he should pull over right now? Maybe, if he doesn't, the tire will pop off and it'll cause a huge wreck. The Terrain starts to close in on the Target logo. Robert checks the left side mirror and is immediately annoyed by the bright, blue lights of a Camry in the left lane. While the badness continues to rustle and swish inside his stomach, the Accord remains close in his rearview. He sits up, eyes darting back and forth between the semi and rearview. His spine is straight, and his seatbelt is tight against his chest. The Camry is now even with the Accord, so Robert can't switch lanes. The Target logo is closing in on his windshield, perhaps a three-second's distance now. He imagines that thick, crunching sound once more, and his heart seems to sink through his torso.

This is getting old, Robert thinks. All the time, he worries about dying. All the time, his mind entertains fantasy-like daydreams about the eulogy for his funeral, the sad and sullen faces at the wake. "He was going to be a great father," some people would say. "Such a kind, responsible young man. Didn't come from much, but he did things the right way." He imagines his bleary-eyed mother standing next to Allie before his casket, receiving the hands of those in line. His father would be standing somewhere behind the congregation, nodding hard and quick at whoever walked inside the funeral home, a hand maybe nuzzling the inner pocket of his suit jacket. He can sense, in his imagination of Allie's colorless, formless face, untold sadness. Surely, it's not good to keep this bottled up inside but—

The semi brakes, its lights demanding concentration. His foot taps the brake ever so slightly to buy some space, but the Accord is now even closer to the Terrain. Robert's tongue presses against the roof of his mouth, teeth clenched, jaw and neck flexed. He pours all of his focus into the task at hand. One mistake and boom—he's a corpse. His wife will be a widow, and his child will grow up without a father. Just *one* mistake, and he'd be no better than his Dad.

He wants to scream right now at the Accord's driver. How can they not realize the gravity of the situation? More rain pelts the

Terrain's windshield. Right as Robert considers brake checking, something he normally would never do, the Accord backs off a bit. Robert shifts in his seat and checks his blind spots. The Camry drives parallel to the Terrain, and the Accord again inches closer. His foot hovers over the edges of both the gas and brake pedals.

Whoever is driving the Accord reminds Robert of Dad's driving. He always liked it more when Mom drove. Even though she was a scared driver, at least she was defensive. Dad, on the other hand, was fearless and aggressive, if not outright dangerous. He remembers the way Steve Acton hunched forward in the driver's seat, the way his long legs margined the steering wheel, remembers his reddened face and pained, toothy grimace. It was obvious in the way he drove that he believed the world ought to make way, that he was not the one at fault, that his lost patience was a sign of an external failure and not an internal one.

A tall, dead tree catches Robert's eye. It races next to the semi, fast and quick. It's a gnarled hand waving.

He hears a honk. It lasts only a second but feels longer. Robert raises his eyes to the rearview. There's no way he's honking at me, he thinks. No *fucking* way. The Accord is as close as it's ever been. Robert can see the driver's hands tightly gripping the wheel and the windshield wipers furiously fending off the rain. The semi brakes fast. Its lights are a menacing, vicious red. Robert flinches, shock coursing through his veins and jarring his muscles as he veers the Terrain to the right. His tires bump over the slats on shoulder. His eyes are locked on the edge of the semi's bumper. He looks nowhere else until the Terrain's left-side grill clears the fatal corner. The semi's brake pads are screeching, spitting their agony into the air. His left-side tires glide over the slats as the right-side tires coast over the grass. He lets off the gas pedal while looking through the window on his left. The Terrain races forward on the shoulder while the semi wobbles erratically in the right lane, brakes still screaming. The semi seems to be shooting backward. He can read the fat, capital letters on its cargo: EXPECT MORE, PAY LESS. TARGET. His shoulders and neck shake with the Terrain's bumpy handling on the grass. His fingers cling tight to the steering wheel while the car decelerates. As the Terrain edges back onto the road, Robert hears the harsh skidding of 18 tires. He accelerates in spite of it, rushes to put that noise behind him, but two loud smacks rise above the skidding. He merges back onto the road, then into the left lane without signaling, right foot heavy. In the rearview, he sees the semi is angled across the width of the entire road. The Accord and Camry did not make it to the other side. The logo on the cargo stares back at Robert: EXPECT MORE, PAY LESS. TARGET. Brake lights in his peripheral bring him back to the road ahead.

Sunlight slips through a gap in the clouds, yet the rain falls harder than ever. Robert's eyes flutter up and down, left and right, as he evaluates the road; his mouth is contorted into a toothy grimace and his nostrils are fully flared. The sudden sun intensifies the whiteness of the clouds. Robert can't shake the badness festering in his gut. It's a tidal wave that never breaks, that only gets taller and darker and heavier as it surges forward, determined to destroy. What if I really messed up the tires, now? Robert asks himself. My suspension? Axles? Further east, dark gray clouds loom above the Indianapolis skyline.

*****

Robert is crying as he sits in the Terrain that evening, but he doesn't know why. Through tears, he studies the brick wall in front of him. It's raining especially hard now, much worse than on his way in. He stayed an extra hour after work today and has been sitting in the driver's seat for 10 minutes already, but he can't make himself buckle in just yet. He gets a vague sense that his crying is synchronizing with something else, with something both far-off and close. And, as if emerging through the fog of his mind, the something becomes his Dad crying. The only time he saw Steve Acton cry was when their dog Marty died.

The memories pummel him, and he releases several moans in quick succession.

"Oh, Marty, no," Robert whimpers in the Terrain. "No, no, I'm so sorry Marty, I didn't mean it."

He slams the butts of his hands into the steering wheel—*bang, bang, bang.*

He sees Steve knocking his skull after he found out, each knock harder and sharper with the crests of his knuckles.

"You think this hurts, Robert? Imagine how Marty felt, you ungrateful little asshole! Who said you could drive my car? *Who,* goddammit!"

"I'm sorry, Dad, p-please, Dad, it was an *accident.* I thought he was inside, I just wanted driving practice, I—"

"I don't give a shit what you thought! You just *killed* a part of our family, Robert. All of us—'cept you—*loved* him. Now he's dead—get back here!"

Robert escaped to his room and locked the door. He sat against the door, his head ringing, for nearly an hour, but Steve never called for him again that night. It was quiet for the first twenty minutes or so, and at one point, Robert even thought he was asleep. He cracked the door open a hair and peered outside. Steven Acton was sprawled on the floor, rocking slightly—crying.

And it was that sound—that pierced wail—that synchronized with Robert's as he sat statue-still in the parking lot of his office, as the rain assaulted the roof of the Terrain.

"Now he's dead," Robert whispered to the steering wheel, eyes shut yet still stuck on the memory. "Now he's dead, now he's dead, now he's dead, he's dead."

III

Robert's eyes feel bone dry at 1:30 on Sunday morning. He's more than a little tipsy as he sips from his fourth Osiris IPA of the night. The chewing tobacco stewing in his bottom lip provides both comfort and nausea. He is watching *The Fast and the Furious: Tokyo Drift* in the recliner, as still as he was three hours ago when Allie went to bed. The television douses him in a pasty-white glare, and the speakers blanket him in tire squeals and surging engines.

He spits again and sighs. Perhaps out of a justifiable spite, Allie left the large Target box containing the baby crib just under the television. It's been sitting there for weeks now. She no longer asks him to build it, just like she no longer asks him to come to bed with her. The bullseye logo taunts him with its red stillness. Part of him wants to wait to make the crib until after they move, but the rest of him knows this is unwise. She's due within the month. They aren't sure which will come first: the pregnancy or the move. The lack of sureness, Robert rationalizes, justifies this paralysis. Right?

There is a part of him, though, that wants to be spiteful. Allie never responded to the photos he sent of the worksite in Brownsburg. Never said a thing. Isn't that visit something significant? Sure, she doesn't know about his fear of driving, but even beyond that, he's trying. His job isn't exactly easy, after all.

Not that being pregnant is easy, though. He shakes his head, peeved that he can't even be peeved. He worries he no longer can do anything right, as Allie has been suggesting:

"All right, Robert, look. Here's what it is. If you're going to keep moping around and not talking to me, if you're not going to pick up your weight around here, I don't think I want you in the delivery room. You can wait outside with our cousins if you're going to be like this. I'm serious." After a few minutes of silence, Allie threw her hands in the air. "Like *this*! *This* is what I'm talking about!" Then she

34

fled to their room and slammed the door shut. He should have said something, he knows now. Letting that kind of comment go un-unaddressed was a big mistake, but now, as he sits in his recliner, he realizes he was just hurt. Inaction, he knows, is his salve.

Robert enjoys watching Sean Boswell do his thing; he loves his every bit of dialogue, his confidence while turning into each drift. They look similar enough, and they sort of even speak the same. He spits into an empty Osiris can. More accurately, Sean sounds like his Dad, both of their drawls bending every syllable. Long ago, Robert polished out the hick in his voice so as to more easily distinguish himself from his upbringing. Unlike his parents, he hates Larry the Cable Guy, and the singing bass, and Indy car racing. He resents that culture because it is a source of pride for his parents, and as far as he is concerned, they shouldn't be proud of anything they represent. They certainly aren't proud of him. But Sean Boswell's drawl evokes an entirely different feeling in him, a feeling he can't quite name as the alcohol and nicotine flare up. He spits again. His parents often mistook his aloofness as stupidity or obstinance. Shows what they know. If they spent even one hour at his job, their feeble brains would break like the overeager racecars on his screen. They would shatter into shards like the Sedan. He spits with malice, imagining their faces at the bottom of the can.

"Couldn't even come to the wedding, huh?" he mumbles to the Osiris, his eyes half-shut. "Couldn't make it to your only child's wedding, you fucking assholes." It dawns on him these are the first words he's spoken aloud since Allie went to bed. And then he remembers he was the one who didn't want them invited, despite Allie's numerous reminders and double-confirmations. "Are you sure-sure?" she asked after the rehearsal dinner. "Like, positive? You don't want to look back on this and regret it, is all I'm saying."

He's shaking his head again. Steve and Lilly Acton had no problem telling their son he was an accident. In fact, they even went so far as to call him a mistake when they were especially angry at their do-good, brown-nose, crybaby son. Not inviting them might have been a mistake. Not that he wants their relationship restored, but the idea of forcing their absence feels vindictive and bitter. Robert doesn't want to be a bitter person. He was always the person who did everything, who never forgot a task, who did every task to the best of his ability. They might have given up on him, but he didn't have to do the same.

To move past the salty tears forming in his eyes, he stands up. His buzz flickers throughout his bloodstream, and he feels flushed

35

along his temples and neck. In the kitchen, he grabs a boxcutter from the junk drawer. He looks at the Target package, once more shakes his head, and sits crossed-legged before it. As he watches the shadows dance along the cardboard, he decides he didn't mind getting called a mistake. Getting called an accident, however, was what hurt the worst.

IV

Exactly two weeks later, Robert is awake at four in the morning on a Sunday. He's researching the safety of U-Haul trucks and explanations of their mechanics. A few hours from now, he is supposed to pick one up in Bloomington so they can start unpacking their apartment. But before all of that, Robert must make sure he won't get into, or cause, an accident. Stacks of dip tins stand tall on the side table by his recliner. The laptop is almost too hot, but Robert doesn't even register the heat. His eyes are locked onto the screen, scouring every cranny for information that might just save his life.

Two hours later, he's asleep in the recliner, but this time the dip was removed beforehand. When he wakes up, it's 7:22. He was supposed to leave for Bloomington 20 minutes ago. He pops up out of the recliner, eyes open wide. He immediately feels something off in the air. It's wet outside, he thinks. Nasty, even. His eyes adjust to light seeping into the living room, and a chill crawls along his arms and the back of his neck. A peek through the blinds reveals thick, velvety fog outside. Everything looks blue, gray, and cold.

Robert moves quietly so as not to wake Allie. After disposing of his mess in the living room, he splashes water on his face in the bathroom. He shakes his head vigorously, smacks his cheeks hard. His reflection in the mirror is a little sad: the bags under his eyes, his unshaved face, even pastier skin. Sleepiness is sinking like an anchor in the back of his head, pulling down his eyelids.

He feels it in his arms and legs as he reverses out of the garage. As the Terrain gently presses forward, he notes more fog has seeped into the neighborhood. It steals between houses, engulfs the sidewalks. Robert can barely make out the trash cans and mailboxes that line the road. He takes a deep breath before turning right.

The neighborhood exit pulls up to a T in the road. Fog obstructs his view on both sides. To the right is the way into town, and to the left is the way to Bloomington. He flicks on his turn signal and pauses.

Robert adjusts each mirror just a touch. He grips his belt, hooks his thumbs over the elastic band of his underwear, and then repositions his clothes to a comfortable fit while raising his butt slightly in the air. Robert thinks about adjusting the placement of his seat but decides against it. He found the perfect orientation weeks ago. Robert watches his knuckles turn white, and he wonders if they too might vanish in the fog's thickness.

The Terrain registers three beeps, and Robert still hasn't turned. He relaxes his face, and he lets his shoulders roll around. Fuck, he thinks, turn signal still ticking, clock now ticking to 7:40. All right; time to go.

He directs his chin to the left, foot off the brake, about to swing over to the gas. His eyes lose focus when thrusting his vision into the fog, but he's not sure if he sees headlights. The Terrain inches forward, spokes slowly cartwheeling along the pavement. Just before he puts more pressure on the accelerator, two full circles of light puncture the fog, racing perpendicular toward Robert.

His tendons snap into action and help lift his foot off the pedal, but in those moments of slow propulsion, Robert considers whether he should gun it onto the road or reverse to let the car pass. His indecision frightens and angers him. Robert's foot is back on the gas pedal, pressing lightly now.

A white GMC Terrain shatters the fog into the wispy shards. The car runs at him like a speeding fiend, impatient for violence. The car hurls its white light onto Robert's window.

He imagines the explosions blooming within the engine. Lurking under the hood, cylinders slide and push; gasoline lurches into sparks, and sparks into flames—all for the consequence of killing Robert. Once the headlights smash into the Terrain's door, the dying will die within moments of its birth. Robert's body will fold, leftward. Then, as the fractured headlights continue to push into his hip, Robert's head and left shoulder will point toward the other driver. Then, immediately after, Robert's head will smash through his window, through the other windshield, and then finally into the airbag that embraces the other driver's body. But Robert will be moving too fast by then. His trajectory will trump the airbag. Their skeletons will collide, and they will die. Their bones will crunch and snap like their seatbelts. Their nerves will send alarms that can't be registered. Force will puppet their useless muscles and broken joints. Their blood will splatter within the highways of their busted veins, the crumbling infrastructures like that of broken cities. Robert shuts his eyes, waits—

But the other Terrain swerves, launches a jarring, fleeting honk. It's over. He watches the white Terrain ease back into the right lane, watches the exhaust pipe regurgitate smoke from the engine's explosions, its darkness quickly fog-swallowed.

Robert realizes he's crying. He cries harder. After a minute, still pressing the brake pedal, turn signal ticking still, he cries even deeper. At the same time, he shifts into reverse. He drapes his right arm over the passenger-seat and clutches the head of the chair. He cuts the wheel as the Terrain backs onto a driveway, then shifts back to drive.

"I can't do it, I can't—" Robert is bawling now. He maintains the wheel even as he wipes hot tears from his face, smearing them on his forearms. He pulls into his driveway, parks. "I can't let myself die, I can't die on them."

He feels a poisonous adrenaline shooting through his jaw and neck. He takes deep breaths and looks around his clean car, feeling as empty as it. As he exits the vehicle, he decides he'll tell Allie everything. He'll tell her about the accidents he abandoned, his anxiety, his fixation on his own death—about Marty. Upon opening the door, he hears Allie screaming from the bathroom.

"Robert?" she calls out. "Is that you? Please, God, tell me that's you."

He's silent and still. He can't move his mouth, but he's wide awake. He listens to the memory of what she just said, studies the fear in her voice.

And then he realizes he's silent, and says, "Yes. Yes, it's me." By that time, he's in the bedroom, looking at the opened bathroom door.

"It's happening, it's happening!" she pants.

He's inside the bathroom, and he sees her laying in the tub with no pants on. Her shirt is tucked up over her large belly, just above the belly button. She looks at him with pleading eyes. He helps Allie stand up. He watches her every moment as she eases into the passenger seat of the Terrain. His left hand supports her back, and his right hand hovers above her thigh as she puts her legs inside. He opens the back door and deposits the hospital bag. At least he put that together.

Robert is barely thinking as he walks over to the driver's side. His eyes are still bloodshot and bleary, and he's breathing steadily through his nose. His heart is pounding, but he doesn't feel the poison anymore. He clicks on his seatbelt.

The Terrain glides through the neighborhood before pulling up to the T once again.

"Robert," Allie breathes, voice steeped in pain. "I'm so glad you're here."

The Terrain comes to a gentle stop. He looks over to his wife, tears returning to his now smiling face. Robert does not hear a crash. He doesn't see a collision. He imagines his child instead. There, he hears life—sees radiance. After checking for an oncoming car and seeing none, Robert turns right and presses firm on the gas pedal; the Terrain powers forward, straightens out, and disappears into the fog.

*****

Three hours later, an hour after Michael Acton was born, Robert is asleep in a chair. He's dreaming.

It's pitch-black outside, around four in the morning. Robert's driving on I-70, heading toward work. No one else is on the road. He's driving frantically while also trying to dial Allie's number on his cell phone. Dead trees swish past him, their gnarled branches reaching toward him like scythes. Wind breaks itself on the Terrain and snarls away in shrill whistles. He has to hear her voice to slow down, but her not answering is starting to freak him out. Every time the call goes to voicemail, he has to increase his speed another five miles an hour.

Robert passes two semis that are parked on the shoulder; shortly thereafter, he passes a rest stop. More semis are parked on the other side of the stop. All of their hazard lights are on, and they also sport bright, neon displays that line the cargos.

The line of semis doesn't end. It grows longer, like a terrible, segmented snake. As soon as Robert realizes this, the semi he just passed turns on its overhead lights. The next one does the same. All of them turn on their brights, and he can hear the engines picking up. In his rearview, Robert watches them all pull onto the road at the same time, and he can make out the drivers: each one is his Dad.

He floors it. The Terrain creates some distance, but they soon catch up. In fact, the numerous Steve Actons are gaining on him. He presses even harder on the gas pedal, and it works, but the process only repeats. The whole time he's trying to call Allie.

"Where's Marty, you son of a bitch?" his Dads say in unison, as if they are all speaking through megaphones. "Don't you hide him from me!"

The Terrain approaches another truck stop. More semis are perched on the shoulder, and Robert knows more versions of his Dad wait ahead for him. At the same time, a mass of fog avalanches along the highway and rain crashes down on the roof of the Terrain. Somehow, the Terrain is able to remain just ahead of the semis, but Robert knows his lead won't last long.

"Allie, I need you to pick up," he screams at his phone. "I need you, I need—oh shit!"

A dog cuts through the fog, darting perpendicular to the road and just missing the Terrain's front bumper. Immediately after, he hears a scream mixed with a moan—it's his Mom.

A Plymouth Reliant darts by even faster than the dog but in the same direction. As if in slow-motion, Robert watches Lilly Acton shouting after Marty, completely oblivious to the Terrain or the fact that she's driving the wrong way. He can't slow down. He's going to hit her door, just like the Camaro hit the Sedan. He can't stop it now, and he can't avoid the army of Steves behind him, either. He lets off the gas pedal, closes his tear-drenched eyes, and waits to be—

He wakes up. He hears crying, crying everywhere. Adrenaline surges through him—rattles his very bones. The delivery room comes into focus, and so does Allie as she sits up on the hospital bed, smiling despite her fatigue. She holds their son with outstretched arms.

There he is: their son crying. Their son rising.

Seasonal

by Sarah Powley

A recently retired English teacher, Sarah Powley grew up in Illinois and has been a resident of West Lafayette, Indiana, for over four decades. She has also lived in Wisconsin (and, briefly, in Connecticut). She enjoys walking in the woods and photographing the natural world.

In the fall, when my father raked the leaves, he'd mound them up in the backyard in an area where he also incinerated garbage. His children (four of us) danced around the cauldron in the dusk, pagans entranced by the burst of flame, and then (I think I remember), we roasted marshmallows in the afterglow. What I remember for sure is burning my notes from 8th grade Ancient History, feeding the pages to the fire in grandiose gestures of defiance. I've been sorry ever since—and the teacher I became is horrified.

It had to have been in November or December of 1957 when this happened. The Ancient History class had ended the previous spring, but I was still nursing a grudge against the Greeks and the Romans and the teacher whose demands on my time had filled a loose-leaf notebook. Yes, it would have been November or December. The last raking. The oaks this time.

I am raking leaves myself today—maples, ash, and redbud—moving foothills of them into the street, forming neat hedgerows along the whole expanse of our double lot, exhausting my arms and back, but satisfying my need for order and accomplishment. No burning these days. Instead, the city asks for leaves to be raked twelve inches from the curb. I enjoy amassing them precisely so that the inevitable slide of green, yellow, orange, and fire-red stays within the mandated border.

My husband and I put barrels out when our kids were little. No burning, but no orderly mounds, either. I remember our girls at five and eight: my husband would pick them up, use them as human tamps to compress the leaves in the containers. Much squealing, much wiggling in his arms. "Again, Daddy! Again!" they'd scream, and he would oblige, hoisting them high and lowering them into the leaves until his arms grew tired and the thrill abated.

When our daughters were a little older, we created enormous leaf piles in the front yard. The girls never seemed to tire of backing up all the way to the edge of the yard where the earth falls away into

41

a ravine and then running pell-mell into the mountain. We heaped the leaves again and again for these gymnastics; afterwards, the yard was sprinkled with the confetti of the crushed ones, the aftermath of celebration.

My across-the-street neighbor is raking leaves today, too. He's using a blower to organize his collection. Stray leaves two-step between our hedgerows or skid up the center of the street in a procession, like seahorses on parade. I pause at the mailbox, put my hand to my waist, do a side bend for relief. He pauses, too, by his mailbox. "This gets harder every year," he says to me. "Yes, yes, it does," I agree, but I think I have the more difficult job for the bigger yard, the more trees. Yet, what do I know about his infirmities? For some years now, he's worn a mask when he rakes, and he moves, it seems to me, more stiffly than he used to.

Today, pulling the rake against an avalanche of leaves in the driveway, another memory surfaces. After the girls had gone off to college and into their own lives, I began taking my high school students to Russia in the early summer and hosting Russian students here in the fall. The Russian teachers stayed with me. One year, too busy with the exchange to rake, I let the leaves accumulate in the driveway until they were more than a foot high. The teachers were eager to help with the clearing, found delight in raking fall to the curb. Novelty was involved—a real American experience. But raking wasn't unknown to them. *Grabli*, they told me gleefully, was the Russian word for rake. Later, when I was in Russia, I happily used one myself to clear winter debris at a teacher's *dacha*. Novelty was involved—a real Russian experience.

My rake grabs the leaves deftly this afternoon, leaving swathes of myrtle abruptly exposed to the light. I will use the blower afterward to clear the bits of broken leaves, these present-day remains reminiscent of confetti but evoking nowhere near the elation of those jumping days. Years ago, we ripped out the yews that were here against the house and replaced them with the myrtle and a serviceberry. I'd had to arm wrestle the branches of the yews to lift them high enough to extricate the sodden, layered leaves that the wind had packed underneath. A blower might have worked, but blowers were beyond our reach then.

There were years after that when we raked alone together, my husband and me. He'd start at one end of the yard, I at the other, and we'd meet in the middle, done in, but satisfied. Some years, when the wind was blowing, we'd be side-by-side, raking in the same direction, taking advantage of the tailwind. He covered more ground; I'd have

42

to hustle to keep up. He was more thorough than I, the scientist in him approaching the task with deliberation, patience, and steadiness. He took charge.

I didn't imagine age would take charge of him.

Or of me.

I can still squeeze behind the generator to handpick the leaves that cluster there, but I'm winded afterward from the contortion. I can still climb down into and then out of the window wells six-feet deep by the side of the house, though recently my husband, recognizing that he will not be the one to clean out the window wells, bought me a ladder for this purpose. I prefer, for now, my own exit route up the railroad ties that line the wells. But these wells are why I stopped using the blower we eventually bought. Too much of fall ended up at the bottom of the wells, making more frequent descents necessary. More chances of my own fall.

My youngest grandson is 8, soon to be 9. During these Sisyphean assaults on the yard, I've been plucking specimen leaves to add to his collection. Linden and cottonwood a few weeks ago; today, mostly maples—the glory of fall. He has his own school notebook to keep: common name, scientific name, location, date. A classic record of time and place.

He doesn't yet know about eternity, universality, or cycles. He doesn't know that the accumulating leaves are an annual reminder of our own lives falling away. But neither does he know that in the accumulation lie our own ancient histories, recorded as memories, bestowing grace upon the fall.

Learning How to Drown
by Joseph Kerschbaum

Joseph Kerschbaum's most recent publications include Mirror Box *(Main St Rag Press, 2020) and* Distant Shores of a Split Second *(Louisiana Literature Press, 2018). His recent work has appeared in* Reunion: The Dallas Review, Hamilton Stone Review, The Inflectionist Review, Main Street Rag, In Parentheses, *and* Umbrella Factory. *Joseph lives in Bloomington, Indiana, with his family.*

Traffic lights flashed slow yellow
    over intersections where no one

crossed paths at that time of night.
    Yield in every direction. Vacant Walmart

parking lot looked haunted, where faint spirits
    drifted under fluorescent lamp posts,

but if you looked close enough, it was
    just August air thick with humidity.

Most households were turned down for the night
    as I drove through the streets

that I could navigate
    with my eyes closed.

Everything felt exotic in the dark
    with no one around.

Police cruisers followed me,
    running my plates for priors

or outstanding warrants. Analyzing my driving
    for signs of intoxication

which was commonplace
    not long before midnight.

The message was clear,
        I wasn't supposed to be there.

Anyone on the streets at that hour
        was suspect somehow.

Thread the needle of driving
        under the speed limit but not so slow

I made my avoidance apparent. No rolling
        stops at stop signs. Gave the bored patrol

no reason to pull me over and find
        the weed in the glove compartment.

Mine was an inverted existence
        where night was my day and day was night,

working third shift as a temp at the plastics factory
        for the summer. Time and my place in it

wasn't clear or linear. I was a tourist
        wandering through lives in progress.

In a few weeks, I would be gone
        on my way wherever

my unfolding path would lead.
        This is why no one bothered

to learn my name.
        Most of the skeleton crew

looked exhausted
        before the shift started.

Still, we had eight mind-numbing hours ahead.
        The brittle thin couple, Amy and Jim,

were androgynous, interchangeable.
        They could pass for twin mannequins

except they walked and talked.
        They were already tweaking

and fidgeting. Most nights,
        they crashed before lunch.

We formed a crescent moon
        around Bill, our mumbling shift manager,

who looked as wrinkled and threadbare
        as his faded flannel shirt.

If Dr. Jekyll had kept a menagerie
        of Mr. Hydes under his skin

and they took turns on the carousel
        of his consciousness, this would be Bill.

There were as many versions of him
        as there were flavors of alcohol

or varieties of narcotics.
        Tonight, it was 'Pills Bill'

who appeared when we clocked in
        then disappeared until dawn.

What reaction is justified after you reach
        the arduous peak of your life

only to realize you were scaling
        a mountain of garbage?

All of this was according to employees
        who mocked Bill,

gossiped in the parking lot,
        and snickered as he called out

who would work each press for the night.
        There was no winning or losing,

all of the machines were equally
tedious and soul-erasing.

Each decrepit press was kept on life support
well beyond its intended lifespan.

They labored heavily as if running in place
with a collapsed lung.

As each machine gave up the ghost
an alarm would ring

like a heartbeat flatlining on a monitor.
With each mechanical breakdown,

a voice that sounded like a refrigerator
thrown down a flight of stairs

erupted in a stream of obscenities.
You could hear the fury of a life wasted

patching together so many things
that wanted to stay broken,

machines or otherwise. Watching that fucking boulder
roll down the same goddamn hill

again and again. Todd, the third-shift mechanic,
was a perpetual ball of rail-thin, grease-covered,

speed-addled, balding rage menacing the factory floor
like a schoolyard bully in steel-toed boots.

The ever-present wrench in his white-knuckled fist
always looked like a weapon.

Each press was an unwilling Lazarus
dragged back to life night after night.

Less a savior, Todd was more of a masochist.
If machines could feel anything,

they would have a shared sense of impermanence
with those of us who occupied the assembly lines.

Together we forged hot plastic
in the shape of big gulp cups.

All summer, all of us made
low-quality promotional plastic products

for an animated movie no one remembers,
sold at a burger chain no longer in operation.

Everything we made was disposable
detritus that had no value

and now overflows landfills.
Anyway, Candy would say, *it's a paycheck.*

Who gives a shit where this garbage goes?
Someone is going to make it,

and might it as well be her.
She was behind on bills,

and her car needed a catalytic converter.
And they didn't do drug screenings,

which is an invasion of fucking privacy
by the way, she reminded me frequently.

What she does in her free time
is none of their goddamn business.

She walked out to Kyla's Ford Focus
where they smoked meth during lunch.

Alone in my Mercury Comet,
I ate a baloney sandwich and sparked a joint.

The sun would rise in a few hours. I would
be gone in a few weeks,

back to state college. Blue-collar, free-lunch,
      food-stamps kid who sold plasma

twice a week to pay for textbooks
      and worked at factories

over breaks to pay tuition. During that long,
      exhausting summer, I felt

misplaced in the world. I was a tourist
      everywhere. I didn't belong anywhere.

Inside the other parked cars,
      red tips of cigarette cherries

glowed in the dark.
      Smoke rolled out of the windows.

Faces gazed out into the night.
      Small embers pulsed with each deep inhale,

thinking about whatever other people think about
      at three in the morning, alone in their car,

when the August heat
      doesn't relent even at night,

just like everything else that stalked
      in the dark at the edges

of the yellow lamp post light.
      One moment of turbulent peace

before heading back
      into the belly of the rusted beast.

At four in the morning, time contorted.
      Early morning hours elongated

like taffy sagging in the middle as it stretches.
      The second half of third shift

always felt twice as long
        as the first half.

Mixed with moderate insobriety, the monotonous
        sound of the machines became a rhythm

that lulled anyone into a dulled existence between
        waking dream and sleepwalking reality.

Operating a press for hours was muscle memory,
        rhythm, and timing. Nothing to do with skill.

Close the metal door, open the metal door,
        pull out eight hot plastic cups,

place them in a box, close the door, open the door,
        hot plastic cups, stack in boxes,

open, cups, box, close, open, cups,
        box, close, open, close, open,

close, open, cups, box, close, open, cups,
        box, close, open, close, open,

close, open, close, open, close, open,
        close, open, cups, box, close.

Urban legend said if you disturb a sleepwalker
        mid-dream, they would be shocked awake

and have a heart attack. This is not true.
        Otherwise, we would have all been casualties

scattered across the factory floor when the bell rang
        at the end of our shift every night.

We walk fatigued out of the building. Jolted
        by sunrise, fresh air that wasn't toxic,

and a rush of nicotine from the first drag
        off the first cigarette in hours.

Cicadas were already stirring up their singing.
　　　Low hum in the morning

with a deafening assault in the afternoon.
　　　As scheduled, their brood returned

after seventeen years.
　　　Staring through her thick sunglasses,

Candy said, *Jesus Christ, has it been seventeen years?*
　　　I started working at this fucking place last time

those disgusting bugs covered everything.
　　　I was a temp worker like you, she said looking at me.

During the summer of the previous Brood X,
　　　Kyla married that cheating piece of shit Rick.

But that was a great summer, she said,
　　　nothing like this one.

In unison, a dozen cars pulled out of the parking lot.
　　　Morning traffic was flowing

in the opposite direction. Nothing exotic
　　　about driving home at sunrise.

The Walmart parking no longer looked haunted.
　　　Daylight had exchanged one kind of ghost for another.

No cops followed me home.
　　　They were perched

under overpasses hunting
　　　for speeders on the interstate.

I smoked one last joint before pulling up
　　　to the duplex rental across from the county jail.

I met my father as he opened the front door,
　　　framed like staring into a mirror

that reflected a future
that waited at the end

of a long road of difficult circumstances
and bad choices.

You'll never know
which ones are the bad ones

until it's too late.
He nodded and said there is still coffee

as he headed out for first shift
at the driveshaft factory.

Rinsed off and laid down, I listened
to the rattle of the electric gate

across the street, open and close as cops
ended and started their shifts.

Woke mid-afternoon in a haze, unsure
if it was morning or evening. All summer,

I existed outside of time and inside a future
that was already waiting,

all I had to do was nothing
and it was ready to begin.

Like learning how to drown;
just stop moving

my arms and legs, don't panic
as the surface disappears.

Or chose to swim until I lose sight
of the shore, until I have no choice

but to keep swimming
out into the bottomless dark.

Re-mapping Zanesville
by Mark Allen Jenkins

Originally from the hilly corner of Ohio, Mark Allen Jenkins's poetry has appeared in Gargoyle, minnesota review, South Dakota Review, Every River on Earth: Writing from Appalachian Ohio, *and* Still: The Journal. *He completed a PhD in Humanities from the University of Texas at Dallas and currently teaches in Houston.*

The Bloomer Candy Company on Route 40 vanished
from Zanesville last year like ice pellets.

Down in Putnam, the part of town that crumbles
like nowhere else, where Harriet Beecher Stowe's brother
once preached, where the Muskingum Pioneer Historical Society holds on
to history, books, photos, stuff people
leave on their front step. My father shows me a giant
hand-drawn atlas of the city
used by a local insurance company to track
loss and risk in commercial property
buildings, factories,
warehouse, houses, schools, churches.
Fire and police alarms.

How many night watchman could sound the alarm against damage?

Elsewhere on the map, building
sized paper is cut, then affixed
for new buildings, old buildings, buildings
gone. Beautiful and archaic, Zanesville today
would need a larger map to cover
the city but also emptier, to not show
the demolished red brick auto parts factory
on Linden next to Anchor-Hocking Glass Molds,
waiting for demolition and a buyer.
My old elementary school, empty of desks and students,
Polk Scrap Iron bought it to park
trucks and hoppers filled with twisted bumpers and beams

Where is the glue to press down the half empty Colony
Square mall, once the new mall, and still the mall when I was
just a short walk away. My parents would take
my three year old self to watch its construction.
Earth movers, bulldozers, truck after truck hauling away hill tops
Exchanging for concrete, bricks, lumber. I couldn't see downtown

Where department stores Sears, JC Penny, and Lazarus
left to join this new construction, more buildings to cover up.

Mapping Zanesville is unsealed road, cracks, breaks
under ice, snow, sun, then weeds. Last summer, Google Maps,
told me to turn right on a non-existent part of my parent's dead
end street. Already, the map
in my head fills up this mistake.

I Smiled at the Angry Cross-Dresser

by David Sapp

David Sapp, writer, artist, and professor, lives along the southern shore of Lake Erie in North America. A Pushcart nominee, he was awarded Ohio Arts Council Individual Excellence Grants for poetry and the visual arts. His poetry and prose appear widely in the United States, Canada, and the United Kingdom. His publications include articles in the Journal of Creative Behavior, *chapbooks* Close to Home *and* Two Buddha, *a novel* Flying Over Erie, *and a book of poems and drawings titled* Drawing Nirvana.

Along Main Street near the art museum, my wife and I pass the angry cross-dresser. I do not ignore him. Politely, intending to be nothing more than cordial, I offer him a little smile and a little wave. I almost say, "Hello." He is wearing an airy pleated to-the-knee skirt in bright aquas and teals. Filmy in the breeze. A simple traditional white blouse. Tiny gold hoops. Today the word "flamboyant" doesn't fit. He selected a prudent mix of solids and florals, nothing any more daring than any other average gal. His hair is cropped short and could have been cut by Mayberry's barber, Floyd. Apparently, he wears no make-up and if he does it is tasteful and restrained, nothing that might detract from fashion. His legs look like mine, unattractively knobby. Though smooth and pale, they appear to be unshaved. Maybe like me, his hair disappears near the ankles from too many years and too many socks—an old man thing. Sheathed in men's clothes, he could be the guy who mixes your paint at the hardware store or the guy at the electronics outlet in blue polo shirt and khakis. And perhaps on workdays, that is the case.

We've noticed him before while lunching at the Corner Café on Professor Street in a loud, short summer sun dress and capped in a smart straw trilby hat with the spare, 1960s brim. Chartreuse green plastic earrings from the Dollar Store. Red high-top sneakers. The dress would be best described as "cute" or "sassy," not "elegant." The print was vivid and fun, and it tied in the back. I could not help but think of my eighth-grade girlfriend as she had a dress like that. He could be a middle-aged mom dressing to match the youth of a teenage daughter. At another time, he strolled along Tappan Square, the college green, in hot pink yoga pants. Flared in the leg. Very revealing on women, these were even more startling clinging to him.

Though wedge sandals might go with either of these outfits, I recall his shoes as sensible if not actually masculine. I would guess evening wear would be a classic little-black-dress with a plunging neckline, a lot of back and of course a string of pearls. Accessorized with a small, chained clutch. What would he wear for a wedding? Did he shop online, at the retro consignment shop downtown, or J.C Penney? His success is in balancing pragmatism and comfort, femininity and identity.

Of course, I could not help but wonder: boxers, briefs, or panties? Mary Alice, an art school chum, wore men's white briefs rather than women's panties. She waved the packages of six at me—her Christmas presents, but I never saw her in them as we were not an item. She preferred BVDs. I was a Fruit of the Loom guy. She was not interested in proffering a manifesto. She simply found men's underwear more comfortable, much more practical and substantial. I always wondered what she thought of the flap in the front, a remnant of ye olde codpiece. I never use the flap, a nuisance, but it is a constant reminder that this particular garment is intended to house male genitalia.

I have a black and white photograph of my dad, a highly closeted gay man who somehow survived a small rural Ohio town in the 1950s—but not a marriage. He is on the set of a high school play seated beside his female friends, posed and attired exactly like the other girls in a modest tea-length skirt (no poodles) and blouse—a spare, tasteful ribbon around his collar. He seems even dowdier than and could easily be Mamie Eisenhower. Though playing a character, his face is telling. He is enjoying not only the attention, but the fabrics. He seems comfortable—at home in his costume.

I smiled at the angry cross-dresser and waved a little wave. I say "angry" as his expression seems to be a consistent scowl, but the scowl is antithetical to the often playful whimsy of his ensemble. And "scowl" is not accurate. I think it is simply a pensive defiance, a determination to be himself. Maybe he prepares each outing for the stares of incomprehension. (As an artist, I understand the gawking. However, nothing I do is as committed as this man's passion.) Each day he readies himself for the possibility of being accosted–abuse hurled at him from a passing pickup truck. Or worse, he girds himself for those that simply but pointedly ignore him. I do not ignore him. Maybe gay, maybe transgender, maybe neither, I don't know and don't assume. Or rather, it is none of my business. And I am pretty sure this is all irrelevant to his unique articulation of fashion. I am simply fascinated with his boldness, his creativity, his canvas, his courageous search for authenticity. You see, I admire him. Though I am not likely to wear a dress any time soon (too old, too homogenized, too much trouble), I hope I might be as fearless.

Jacob's Painting
by David Sapp

Jacob wore big plastic dayglo green earrings to match a grandmother's housecoat he wore as a dress, a yellow and chartreuse print muumuu. He was unlike any other student in my painting class. He reminded me of Chris Farley or maybe Jonathan Winters cutting up Johnny Carson on *The Tonight Show* fifty years ago. Everything about Jacob was big—his personality, his laugh, his generosity. His sarcasm was enormous, loud, and harmlessly savage. It had to be. He was out, largely so, long before it was acceptable to be gay at this little college, long before LGBTQ was a household acronym, before they/them was a preference, before Obergefell v. Hodges, when it was dangerous to be proud of his identity, never mind outspoken in this backward, rural town.

For the fourth portfolio assignment, he created an abstract shaped painting constructed of two by twos, plywood, and stuffed with second-hand clothes from the thrift store to give it form–all covered with stretched canvas. (I later wondered if Jacob intended any symbolic significance in using clothing or whether the method was simply an inexpensive convenience.) It was sealed in white gesso primer then painted in bold, almost garish colors. It was Jacob. It was beautiful. It was beautiful because it was Jacob. I acquired Jacob's painting for the college and together we hung it proudly in an empty hall on an empty white wall. I passed it nearly every day going to classes.

Twenty years later, after losing track of Jacob, the maintenance crew removed the painting, misplaced it, and thoughtlessly tore a hole in the canvas during a renovation. You could see part of a shirt sleeve and the buttons of a sports jacket through the opening. When I eventually found the painting and discovered the damage, I was nearly fired, nearly perp-walked off the campus for hurling exquisite expletives in the halls—aimed at no one in particular as no one would fess up. No one seemed to know or see anything. No one was remorseful. (I would have gladly welcomed a simple "sorry about that" from anyone.) A committee was called, a meeting convened. I was admonished for my behavior. A reprimand was issued. And the painting simply vanished. There was an unspoken understanding: no one was to inquire about the disappearance of Jacob's painting.

Around the corner, there's a drawing of a surrealistic landscape by Mike, who would go on to get his MFA; a quiet still-life by the odd and shy Ava; a wood relief by Autumn, the gal who changed her own brakes and repaired her own plumbing; a print by Jeff, who died of lung cancer; a painting emulating O'Keeffe by Phyllis, a concert flutist until arthritis; Andrea's etching, a quirky depiction of her parents with their camper; pictures by Liz and Taylor—they were always seen together at receptions and I called them Liz Taylor. Now, when I pass the empty wall, the empty hall where my memory of Jacob's big personality once hung for everyone to enjoy and admire, I mourn his absence.

Jeremiah's Beach
by Joy Riggs

Joy Rigs is the author of the nonfiction book Crackerjack Bands and Hometown Boosters: The Story of a Minnesota Music Man. *Her essays have appeared in publications including* Hippocampus, The Manifest-Station, HerStry, *and the* Star Tribune. *She lives and writes in Northfield, Minnesota. You can read more of her work at joyriggs.com.*

Anne parks the rental car in the crowded lot, and we saunter toward the ocean, past an ice cream truck, letting our heartbeats slow after the 75-minute drive through the mountains and around the bay on narrow, curvy roads. It's a sunny day in early August. The stiff breeze from the North Atlantic makes me grateful for my light jacket. According to my phone, it's 63 degrees Fahrenheit. Since we are in Ireland, I should be thinking in Celsius, but sadly, those metric system lessons in third grade never stuck.

Anne sports sunglasses and an emerald-green wool hat she bought two days ago at a cute shop in Dingle town, and she has a swimsuit on under her clothes. I'm wearing a Guinness ball cap and no sunglasses, and my swimsuit is in a bag inside the car, just in case. I squint at the patches of bright blue sky, which peek out through low-hanging puffs of white and gray clouds, as we follow a paved path and descend half a dozen concrete steps to the expanse of sand beyond.

The view stops us in our tracks. Although we are first cousins born three months apart, and not identical twins, we gasp in unison. "Wow."

"It's gorgeous. Gorgeous!" Anne exclaims.

A rush of pleasure engulfs my body, like a wave hitting the shore. It's like I'm immersed in a panoramic movie—like those Circle-Vision 360° movies at Epcot in Disney World—except it's real. To our left, facing south, the white-gold sand beach, or strand, stretches for seven miles (I know this because I'd looked it up during my pre-trip research). Where the beach meets the water at the horizon, purple mountains rise into the clouds, and the line of mountains extends from the south to the west; these mountains, which we drove through, are located on the Dingle Peninsula, our home base for most of this week. To our right, or facing north, modest one- and two-story buildings nestle between ocean and the green slope of the Kerry head peninsula. If I look closely, I can make out the gray stone ruins of a castle we passed on the way to the parking lot. This castle only dates back to 1812, but it was built on the site of a previous castle that was raided by pirates in the 1700s. Ghosts supposedly haunt the newer structure, which was set on fire in 1921 during the Irish War of Independence, and now houses both a private residence and a public 9-hole golf course.

"Should we walk down the beach a ways?" Anne asks.

"Yes, let's."

The tide is out, and we veer south and west, toward the water's edge. I step around small shells, clumps of seaweed, and worm-like markings in the sand; a sign we later spot near the parking lot explains that the markings are worm casts—heaps of soil excreted by worms that burrow underground.

We also step around a white circular blob the size of a Frisbee; this giant alien eyeball is my first-ever sighting of a jellyfish in the wild, a reminder that danger often lurks amid beauty in this land of my ancestors.

Anne and I pass families on holiday, people with dogs, kids flying a kite and making a sandcastle. There are no matching chaise lounges here, no servers bringing drinks with umbrellas in them. Ballyheigue is not that kind of beach.

Anne remembers being here once before, as a child, with her four older brothers, her dad, and her mom, Mary (who was my mom's oldest sibling). This was in the early 1970s, when Anne's dad was stationed overseas; her main memory of the experience is seeing a dead shark that had washed up on the beach. But this is my first trip to the birthplace of my Irish great-grandfather, Jeremiah Falvey.

A dark-haired woman in her 20s, wearing a bikini, strides past us, her skin wet from her dip in the ocean.

"How is the water?" Anne asks.

The woman smiles. "The water is actually warm; it's the air that makes it seem cold."

Back in Minnesota, Anne is fairly introverted, as am I, but since we arrived in Ireland she's been chatting up locals like a politician seeking votes. I find it endearing that she's enthusiastically embracing her Irish roots, even though she's only Irish on her mom's side. I have the same Irish genes Anne has, from our shared grandfather (plus a smidge from our shared grandmother); according to my DNA test, I am—to borrow a phrase from superstar performing artist Lizzo—35 percent that Irish lass.

Anne turns to me. "I'm going to go back to the car and get a towel. Do you need anything?"

Thinking of the jellyfish, and the air temperature, I shake my head. "No thanks, I'm good. I'll wait here."

While Anne is gone, with my iPhone, I attempt to capture the visual parfait of colors before me: a horizontal layer of gold sand streaked with reddish-brown seaweed, topped by white surf, blue-green water, purple mountains, blue-gray sky, finished with a dollop of marshmallow clouds.

I will post the photos later on Facebook for my 82-year-old mom, who never had the chance to meet her paternal grandfather or visit this town where he was born, 158 years ago—a town he left at age 19, for greater opportunities in the United States.

"How could he leave this beautiful place?" Anne asks when she rejoins me near the water and strips off her layers.

I consider what I know of Jeremiah: he immigrated in 1888 to the south side of Chicago. He took a job as a laborer and met and married Mary Therese Costello, who immigrated from the nearby seaside town of Ballybunion, just 15 and a half miles—or 25 kilometers, for the metric fans—north of where we are standing. Anne and I had been there the day before, visiting a handful of our Irish cousins.

"Things must have felt pretty desperate," I say.

Before our trip to Ireland, Anne read several books and watched numerous movies about Ireland. I didn't do the historical research Anne did, but I did know what I had never learned as a kid: a million Irish didn't have to die in the potato famine; local farmers produced other crops, but under British rule, the government continued to export large quantities of food out of the country.

My family research has not yet yielded clues about Jeremiah's specific reasons for leaving, which was 30 years after the Great Famine. I knew it wasn't easy for them in Chicago, either. Mary T. worked as a maid, cleaning houses along Lake Michigan. Their first two children died as infants. They had five more children in quick succession, all boys; my grandfather was No. 4. Jeremiah opened a bar that became successful, but because his wife had "trouble with the drink," as my Irish cousins would say, the family left the city first for a farm in rural Iowa, and then for one in rural Minnesota, before settling in St. Paul.

Jeremiah died a year before my mom was born. Mary T. lived for several more years, but because she and my grandmother—her daughter-in-law—didn't get along, my mom has no memories of time spent with her Irish grandmother.

In a photo taken a few years before Jeremiah's death, he has a jovial grin and a sparkle in his eyes; he looks like he would have been fun to know. His wife, Mary T., on the other hand, a stocky, unsmiling woman with a gray bun in her hair, looks like she's been through some things.

I take off my socks and hiking shoes, roll my jeans up to below my knees, and walk toward the waves. The sand feels both firm and soft; it will surely do wonders to smooth the rough skin on my feet, which have been logging more than 13,000 steps a day since we arrived in the Emerald Isle.

Anne ventures into the water, farther down the beach. I let the waves lap at my toes, breathe in the briny air, and stare out at an ocean view that likely resembles what Jeremiah would have seen as a boy; how many times did he think of his childhood home, once he'd moved to Chicago, or later, when he moved to Minnesota with his wife and five sons? What do our bodies retain of the molecules of our homeland?

When Anne finishes her brief swim, we FaceTime with my mom. Minnesota is seven hours behind us, and Mom is still in bed, but I want her to know I'm thinking about her; today is the birthday of my older sister Michele, who died of SIDS when she was six months old. Mom will turn 83 next month; her father died when she was only 13, and her mother has been gone for more than 30 years. She has outlived all three of her siblings, including Mary.

Mom almost died when she gave birth to me; she underwent surgery and chemotherapy for ovarian cancer at age 56, when I was pregnant with my first child; and a year and a half ago, she had a lumpectomy and radiation for breast cancer. I marvel at her resilience. Despite all she's lost, she has kept her sparkle, and her ability to laugh through her tears.

The older I get, the more I appreciate my own tendency to find humor in the darkest of situations. How else does one cope? "It's because we're Irish," Mom says.

On the walk back to the car, I carry four souvenirs in my coat pocket: a creamy white, scalloped shell with a purple stripe, and three smooth stones the size of almonds—one black, one white, and one golden yellow. They are all for my mom, a gift from Jeremiah's beach.

Reflections in Abandoned YMCA

by Marshall Smith

Marshall Smith is educated in the art of creative writing, and specifically poetry, at the world-famous University of Iowa Writers Workshop MFA program. Marshall's book, The Truest Thing I Know, *will be published by Pegasus in the summer of 2024. Marshall studied under Pulitzer Prize poet Donald Justice, and poets Marvin Bell, Stephen Dobyns, and Sandra McPherson. Marshall has taught creative writing classes and seminars, is on the steering committee for the Kenosha Writers Guild, has been a speaker on behalf of the Wisconsin Writers Association, and is published in various anthologies. After having grown up and lived in the Chicago area, Marshall and his wife, Katherine, now live by Lake Michigan in Pleasant Prairie, Wisconsin.*

Photos of old friends
curling in collage
on a bulletin board

doll fraying in her beige dress
lying in broken glass
on a dirty floor

this empty swimming pool
with gang graffiti
fading on a tile wall

an empty shampoo bottle
rolling in the wind
a pink t-shirt and sneakers

in sprung rusty lockers
spilled paint in the shower
splotched peeling musty

a second-place tennis trophy
alone on a shelf in the office
its golden racket brown

when we stop and stare
are there echoes
calling to us

through time's inner ear
like our mothers
in early summer evening

calling for dinner
walking across the clipped lawn
we see remnants of lives

our very own ghosts
walking through houses
doors closing quietly

the many vacant rooms
where we at one time
may have lived

outside's the sough
of twilight rain the hush
of something we can't name

halcyon days in season they were
when the mortgage was paid
every month on time

the car almost new
with its electric windows
my father seen weekdays

in his white shirt and tie
walking with purpose to the train
and now the first days

of summer come
with fantasies of homeruns
and toads in the garden

smells of fresh mud
after rain
the neighbor's mown lawn

contrails dispersing
in the deep blue above
a new moon rising

an early glimpse
into something I believed
would go on forever

Wait

by Miles Varana

Miles Varana's work has appeared in Typehouse, The Penn Review, *and* Passages North. *He has worked previously as a staff reader and managing editor at* Hawai'i Pacific Review. *Miles lives in La Crosse, WI, where he works in journalism and does his best to be a good Millennial despite disliking tandem bike rides.*

Wait:
in the empty shopping malls of Iowa
for the heat to come swinging over the
prairie, wild indigo lolling in the long
afternoon like a twentysomething with a
vape and a Whitelaw refreshing Gmail,
desperate for Seattle, San Diego, Atlanta.

Wait:
on the needled beaches of Ohio, for
more refreshing flotsam to reach your
feet, watching Christmas tree ships
slide their way from Detroit down to
Cleveland. This is your life in Middle
America, one night of Catan to the next.

Think:
in the anesthesia of summer, of this
heartland of irony and theft, of the
ode you write with your minivan;
mayo salad, James T. Kirk, Kwik Trip
sushi. The latticework flatness of this
world touches your smallest fears.

Wait:
to stay, to try to live again.

Farmer and the Dell

by Pella Felton

Pella Felton is a PhD student in the Department of Theatre and Film at Bowling Green State University.

Adam was wrong. That summer in 2003, when he suggested you work for him, on the old Hamlin Farm outside Ludington, on the Michigan side of the lake, near the Sauble Resort. He said you would like it. With its picturesque shores and bucolic pastures. At first you were resistant to spend your junior summer working on a shithole farm town. Away from your friends. And your Anime. And your Livejournal. And your Myspace. And reruns of the *Dawson's Creek* and AOL Instant Messenger. And your collection of 21 mp3s. But I told you that farming is important. It's part of your roots. You came from cow people (people who raise cows, not half-person half cows). But then you found out there was a beach, and I told you if you were good, I'd take you to see John Mayer at the Barrymore at the end of the summer.

In retrospect, I must admit, I thought John Mayer would be better live. And I was still overwhelmed by your curiosity towards boys, my divorce from your mother Lisa, and the fallout from the death of Dale Earnhardt and the September 11 terrorist attacks. You just seemed so sad. No matter how hard you tried, you couldn't conceal the pain I saw in your eyes. Although, I'm not sure how hard you tried to conceal it, cause when you put on LiveJournal that your current mood is "catatonic fugue" people get concerned. Yes. Fine. I read your blog. I like to support independent journalism, and sure, lyrics to Jewel songs and pictures of Snape aren't exactly journalism, but neither is *Drudge.* Because I wanted to know how you were doing. That's why. And I didn't know what to do. I just wanted you to be happy.

I remember the day when I picked you up that August, down the curvy dirt path off East Victory outside of Ludington, Wisconsin. The sky was full of birds, flying through open air like flying birds (what do you want from me? You're the poet. I'm an actuary). Anyway, when I picked you up, I was not expecting the loss of a girl for a quieter, happier woman. Wearing lace up jeans under her JLO skirt, where once there was a girl in belly chains and jeweled fedora.

I remember, you…you looked at a cow you had named "Eve," and you looked at her with an intensity I've never since seen in your eyes. You said goodbye, knowing you would never see her again. You seemed calmer though. More worldly, even at peace, and the money you earned that summer paid for your first desktop computer. A Dell.

Then, we got to the ferry, and you described enthusiastically the process of milking a cow, in pornographic detail for almost two unbroken hours, as if you were reading from a Henry James novel for the first time. Or one of those Linda Howard books you see in the back of stores, that your mother kept on her bedside table. And I was "pleasantly" surprised. Pleasantly surprised when you invited me to a poetry reading held by the Forensics Club in which you described enthusiastically the process of milking a cow in pornographic detail. For four unbroken minutes.

And I will admit as far as cow milking poems go, it remains among the better ones I've heard. Eve (could probably give Janet Jackson a run for her money). You made that cow sound good. I was simply not ready to know that the sound Eve makes when a mother's milk sprays into the yellow plastic bucket is exactly the same as the hot jets which jettison the buttocks upward on the new slide at Crawdaddy Cove Water Park, inside the Holiday Inn West.

I remember that in that cow poem, entitled "Flowers in the Meadow," we learned the cow was called Eve Bunting, as you gave her our last name. Not just because you saw her as a sister, but because she was an innocent. Like you. And had been abandoned. Like you. On the edge of discovering her womanhood. Like you. But also because bunting reminds the mother to release milk.

But the poem went on. And on. And on and on. And the audience started to wonder: "How long till this nightmare is over?" And you told us about losing your virginity to a farmhand named Homer Pickles in a blueberry field to the sound of distant moos. It awakened something deep in you, and then something about the musical *Rent*, which was lost on me at the time.

But then you looked deep into the audience's soul and locked eyes with me, as you asked every person in the room one by one if we would milk you the same way you milked Eve…And let me be clear: I respect your body and your right to choose. But what I never understood, in that moment of unbroken eye contact, was this central metaphor: Eve Bunting was a cow. And you. Sarah Bunting. You're a beautiful young woman who likes watching *90210* reruns, true crime shows, and hates raisins. I still don't know if you wanted us to milk you or not.

I switched to soy milk shortly thereafter.

And I didn't think about it, until that summer when you came home, after Lisa died, and we ordered Papa Johns for dinner. I remember, we stopped by the Blockbuster in Sun Prairie, and we rented *Even Cowgirls Get the Blues* on VHS. We agreed that it wasn't at all what we expected. But we still kind of liked it, and then we both got incredibly quiet before we walked into separate rooms and didn't talk till the next day.

And I remember when you brought home Steve, who I assumed was your new boyfriend with frosted tips and a winning smile. But instead, Steve was just a heifer with considerable bulk and large black spots. You had raised it in the FFA, Future Farmers of America. Steve didn't have a last name. I think he was just a rebound from Eve. But that autumn we sold Steve at the Mifflin Street Block Party to a drunk yuppie who was John Norquist, and we never talked about that again either. I assume he was delicious.

I just wanted you to be happy. That's all I ever wanted.

But that Thanksgiving, you asked me to look at your Dell desktop computer so that you could play Diablo 2, and I saw a Deviant Art Page, on your Netscape Navigator window, with hundreds of pictures of cows. Being milked. And milked. And milked. Cartoons cows. Photos of cows. Cows with human faces. Humans with cow faces. A cow with the head of the cow and the body of a cow. Cows with tentacles. Cows with testicles, which I later learned are called bulls. Cows kissing Sonic the Hedgehog, from the popular video game series of the same name. A .MOV file titled: 2Heffs 1 Bucket. And a cow forever seared into my memory, in a hot pink bodysuit with humanoid buttocks and breasts and the caption, "Your Body Is a Wonderland. Enjoy the Dannon Difference." I walked slowly away from the computer, saying nothing, gave you back your desktop, and threw out the yogurt in the house.

Through all of this I was confused and disturbed, but I did not judge, and I will not judge. I just want you to be happy.

So now, here we are on this Christmas, the great festival of lights. The celebration of the birth of our lord and savior Jesus Christ, in the year of the Lord 2023, we sit together in a dimly lit apartment, watching *the Simpsons* and eating blueberry pancakes, like so many Christmases before. I tell you that Adam has finally sold his farm in Ludington to the Lundberg brothers. You furrow your brow for a second, and I can almost smell Eve's ghost dragging manure in from the afterlife, and you ask me If I'm okay with you being a lesbian.

And I think of all that has passed. In those 20 years. Of You and Eve. And Adam. And Steve. And Homer. And Lisa. And the Johns (Mayer, Papa, and Norquist respectively). And Rain Phoenix, from that Cowgirl film. And those other movies with Don Johnson's daughter, *The Marvelous 30 Shades of Mrs. Grays*, or whatever they're called. Or that show with Zendaya your cousin Bessie watches that keeps me up at night. Or that time I called you to explain "Kink Shaming" to me, when it showed up in the *New York Times* Crossword Puzzle. And those GODDAMN PICTURES, with their drooping cow nipples and asymmetrical cow teats, sliding around below their cow bellies, like cow butter in a cow skillet, and thrusts of a small cow head against cow udders, flapping around like goddamn cow pancakes. And how you turned those *Dawson's Creek* reruns into a career in podcasting. And now your partner, Adele, who clearly loves you, and you clearly love her, and you want to bring into our family.

I look into your eyes, round like saucers of milk, and I think of all we've been through together...And I just...I know I've said this before, but I just want you to be happy. All this time. The years you weren't talking to me. The years I was drinking. The years things got bad. The good times. All of it. I just want you to be happy. And I thought I knew what would make you happy, but I didn't. Even as a baby, you wouldn't drink formula no matter how much I tried; it had to come from Lisa. And some of those years, when I was gone, I felt ashamed that I didn't do enough for you because I didn't know how to be happy. How was I supposed to know that this was what you wanted all along? And sure, I was pretty fucked up on Yaeger for a lot of those years so maybe it didn't happen EXACTLY how I remember it, but today in this apartment, behold, I bring you good tidings of great joy. I am five years sober, finally at peace, and I want to start over.

"Daddy?" you ask.

I wait till the "shhh" at the end of *the Simpsons* credits, take a long sigh, look up from my recliner, and say with all my heart:

"Sweetie, I will ALWAYS love you for whoever you are. I want you to be happy."

Then you look at me, laugh, and say with perfect timing:

"Jeez, Daddy. Don't have a cow, man. Dude. You're getting Adele."

Merry Christmas, Buntsy. Who's ready for eggnog?

The Write Story
by William Thatch

William Thatch is a 14-time published author of short stories in anthologies from Scout Media and Pixie Forest Publishing, and a novella published by Zombie Pirate Publishing. William attributes much of his ability to develop well-crafted, realistic characters to his lived experience facing seemingly insurmountable struggle, and his affinity for professional wrestling, which has afforded him employment as a transcriptionist. William is currently working on his first novel, tentatively titled The Wayward Son. To find out more about William, or get updates on his writing endeavors, visit WilliamThatch.com or follow him on Twitter @IAmThatch.

My name is Ted Allen. If that name sounds familiar, you're probably thinking of the host of those cooking shows; the guy that wears glasses and tennis shoes. I'm not him. I wish I were. The amount of money in my bank account would undoubtedly be much higher.

Alas, I'm a simple man with a simple life. I married my high school sweetheart, Megan, shortly after we graduated. Since then, we have grown our family to two teenagers who hate me—Bryson and Candice—and one toddler who adores me, Louise. We live in the suburbs of Jefferson City, Missouri, in a lovely two-story house with a fat basset hound whose job is to keep the couch from floating away and occasionally soil the carpet. I named the dog Frankie. Frankie only responds to the name "Boner." The oldest children were in that phase where they'd giggle incessantly at the word boner. But more about my family's Boner later.

By my nature, I am a storyteller. I have always enjoyed telling stories. These days, I tell stories as the Senior Underwriting Specialist for Commercial Property and Casualty Lines for the Boreing Insurance Company. "Insurance isn't meant to be interesting" is our motto, and I tell you, there's never an exciting day at the office. Usually, the stories I tell involve my latest trip to the dentist, or about how their insurance policy doesn't cover the recent flood.

On this particular morning, I went through my usual routine—up by six to brush my teeth, a regular bowel movement, and shower. By a quarter to seven, I was seated at the kitchen table eating my usual breakfast of unsweetened oatmeal. With only the family dog awake at this hour, I waved to Frankie.

"Be good today, Frankie," I told him.

Frankie huffed, annoyed I had bothered his essential duty of ensuring the rug did not suddenly become sentient and run away.

I had no sooner reached for the front door to exit when the kitchen phone rang. Deciding I could afford one delay before I had to get going, I answered it.

The voice on the other end brought me back to a time in my life I thought I had put behind me for good.

"I have told you before never to call me at home," I said sternly. "Had I known that was the kind of establishment I was walking into, I would have never entered. No, The Cockpit is not an obvious nightclub name; I thought it was a travel agency. I tipped the gentleman that much because I was told they would take me to pleasures I'd never been to. I thought he meant Branson, Missouri. Yes, I found it odd that the wait staff wore revealing clothing, but I thought it was casual Friday. Now don't call again, Enrique. I hope your mother is doing well. Goodbye."

I returned the receiver to its cradle and took a deep, steadying breath. Memories of the night played in my head. I was still washing glitter out of cracks and crevices I didn't know my body had.

No sooner had I stepped out of the kitchen than the phone rang again. I had time for one more minor delay. But they'd have to make it quick. If I spent more time with delays, I would arrive on time.

Placing the receiver to my ear again, I heard a voice from another time in my life that I thought I had closed the book on for good.

"Theodore! How's my favorite client?" asked the gravely, cigarette, and scotch-ravaged voice.

It was Maurice LaRoux, my agent. I hadn't spoken to Maurice in nearly twenty years, not since my last attempt at a novel had gone without interest from any publishing houses. It was my third novel, and the two which had gotten published were "abysmal failures," as Maurice put it. Heartbroken, I decided that publishing wasn't for me.

"Maurice?" I asked.

"Yes, yes," she said. "I'm so sorry I haven't called in a while. I've been terribly busy."

"For twenty years?"

"A lot happens in twenty years. I got married."

"Congratulations!"

"Then he died."

"I'm so sorry."

"I also got lung cancer," she said, the distinct sound of a Zippo lighter clicking open as she said it.

"That's horrible! Are you going to be okay?"

"I've had it for ten years. God's gonna have to try a lot harder if He wants to kill me. Anyway, did you hear the news? Your first book is selling like hotcakes."

My heart leapt in my chest. It's a medical condition; it happens when I get too excited.

"You don't say?" I said.

"I do say. People noticed the similarities between the plot and that train derailment in Ohio earlier this year, and they can't keep it on the shelves."

The Train That Couldn't Stay On the Tracks—my first novel—had been a thriller about a man doused in the chemicals from a train derailment. The plucky young protagonist, Steve, had to find a way past the police quarantine before things got worse while being hunted. That's called conflict. Stories usually have conflict. Stories without conflict tend to be boring. Have you ever been to a dinner party, and someone told you about the time they met Gary Busey in the supermarket? Boring. No conflict at all. Just a crazy man shopping for watermelons.

"That's great news," I said.

"It is. Some people are still complaining; said it was unrealistic."

"How so?"

"Well, in your book, the government did something about it."

Ba-dum-tssh.

"The reason I called; with all this interest in your work, I thought we should strike while the iron is hot. Announce a brand new Ted Allen novel."

"That is a marvelous idea. I still have the old manuscript that never got sold."

"I was hoping for something less...shitty."

"...well, tell me how you *really* feel, Maurice."

"It was a piece of shit premise from a second-rate writer who rehashed his other two novels."

"I was joking, Maurice."

"I'm not. Anyway, think about it. Come up with something fresh, something new, and get back to me."

I told Maurice I would think about it and get back to her.

For twenty years, my drive to work has been the same. Left turn here, right turns there, get on the freeway, don't make eye contact with the beggars beneath the underpass. The same radio station played the same oldies but goodies. The only difference today was I found myself engaged in creative thinking, trying to find something exciting to write about.

Stories are always about something. They have to be. Otherwise, what's the point? There has to be murder, or a mystery, or family dynamics. Maybe it's about a treasure hunt. Sounds silly to me, but some people are into that. Who? Weirdos, that's who. But even weirdos don't want a string of unrelated events taking place. No one wants to watch a show about nothing. It's simply not done.

My best story ideas always followed the same basic premise. A guy does a thing and gets chased by another guy. In my first novel, a man gets doused in chemicals and chased by police. My second novel was about a guy getting doused in seven secret herbs and spices and chased by a Kentucky Colonel. Though unpublished, my third novel was about a guy who gets doused in honey and chased by bees.

As I drove over the river, it occurred to me water could be used in many ways in a story. That was when I came up with my next great novel idea—*The Man Who Couldn't Dry Off* by Ted Allen, a story about a man who gets doused in water.

I ran through the questions in my head. Why can he not just air dry? Why does he not just change his clothes? Why is he perpetually wet?

After another minute of thinking, I realized Maurice was right. I had developed a formula and was rehashing it once again. I needed something fresh, something new.

I began choosing random things I could see and then trying to create a story from them, such as trees. Cats got stuck in trees. Children climbed trees. Trees were a sign of the season. I considered doing a story from the perspective of a tree, but the concept felt wooden.

Get it? Wooden? I should write a comedy.

I went through this with a few other things I saw. Exit signs on the highway—too boring. A dog walking with a man along the highway—it'd been done. Growing somewhat frustrated, I glanced around my car for something a little closer to home, as it were. That was when I remembered Megan complaining that the car was too small. Trying to drive the entire family, but it was too small. But by myself, I didn't notice.

"That's it!" I exclaimed to myself.

The Man in a Car by Ted Allen. A man decides to escape his problems by living in his car and driving everywhere. Nomadic.

Isolation. Perhaps a bit of madness as highway hypnosis sets in. The car could be a metaphor for locking oneself away from society using technology.

No, that's a Gary Numan song.

This continued until I pulled into the parking lot of the Boreing Insurance Company. The office hadn't changed in twenty years. The portrait of the owner, Bob Boreing, greeted everyone as they walked in. The office had plain, dark grey carpet, the walls blank and white. It was the typical sterile work environment where being different was discouraged—a fantastic environment for thinking about creative endeavors. Everything was a blank slate: no distracting motivational posters or living plants.

I made the rounds wishing my colleagues a good morning and making small talk about the weather and local sports teams as people settled in for a day of filing paperwork and reading other paperwork. Around the water cooler, Janice caught us up on the latest reality television show she was watching. Whenever one of us would walk past Jeff's desk, we would hear him mutter to himself about his gambling debt.

"I'm twenty grand in the hole," he would tell us. "I haven't told my wife yet. What am I going to do?"

"No matter what you do, don't make any drastic decisions," I said with a wink and a nod. "Insurance policies don't cover suicide."

I laughed. Everyone in earshot laughed. Jeff cocked his head as if he had come up with an idea. But he didn't share it. All for the best, really. An office is no place for creativity.

During the lulls of the day, my mind would wander back to the topic of my next great novel. You know what the literary world needs more of? Stories about working in an office setting. There are a thousand and one books about charming, witty secret agents saving the whole world while sleeping with multiple beautiful women and wizards in schools that invariably become the chosen ones for some epic confrontation with the bad guy. I even read one book that merged both of those concepts.

"I have no idea what this author was thinking," read one of its reviews. "But it was still a better love story than Twilight."

I then came up with a great new story idea and a whole new genre I was certain would sweep the literary landscape.

Office Noir by Ted Allen. A gritty look at the world of insurance through the eyes of a world-weary insurance salesman as he fights his way through suffocating plumes of cigarette smoke and the scent of stale coffee to make sure his paperwork gets done.

I wrote notes throughout the rest of the workday when there was time, but I had lost interest by the end. I kept the notes just in case I regained interest. A good writer never throws his notes away. You keep dozens of notebooks filled with ideas you will never look at again. You might have a gold mine waiting in there, but you never want to confirm how terrible most of it is.

On the way home, I stopped at the supermarket to pick up a few supplies for the weekend. As I wandered the store, I wondered if a supermarket would be an interesting place for a story.

Nuclear Bites by Ted Allen. A small group finds shelter from nuclear fallout in the local supermarket.

How would they get enough food? Well...I guess they're in a supermarket. There's plenty to eat. But what about water? ...Yeah, there's a lot of water in there, too. Not ideal. But how would they go about using a restroom? Probably just the employee's toilet. Or a cash register.

Another stupid idea.

Was it always this hard to come up with a story? Looking back on the first novels, I was sure I had come up with the ideas and began writing them in rapid succession. There wasn't much time to think when the story just poured out of you. Perhaps I was rusty. It had been several years, after all.

It was just a matter of attrition to knock the rust from my creative cogs; I just had to keep conceptualizing grocery-based ideas.

The Grocery Gambit by Ted Allen. A man must navigate a treacherous supermarket, filling his cart with groceries at lightning speed; otherwise, it explodes.

No, that's too absurd.

DECLINED! by Ted Allen. A man is forced to pay for the grapes he ate and didn't pay for, but when his credit card gets declined, he isn't allowed to leave.

I think that's called unlawful imprisonment.

Dismayed, I paid for my stupid, unhelpful groceries and got on my way. Some things aren't meant to be stories. On the way home, I contemplated other ideas based on things I saw. Still, I kept running into the same problems—bad location, poor plot, awful lead protagonist, too unrealistic, not unrealistic enough.

As I pulled into the driveway, I put the thought of the novel out of my mind. I had to tend to the family's needs before I could attend to myself. Family must come first. After a quick chat with Megan, wherein I was informed I had neglected to pick up some medication for Candice, I made another quick drive into town.

By the time I returned home, Candice and Bryson were arriving home from school. I met them in the yard and held out the bag with her prescription.

"Here you go, honey," I said.

"Thanks, dork," she replied, snatching it from my hand.

"What did you two learn while you were in school today?" I asked as they walked past me without so much as a greeting.

"That you're a dork," Bryson said.

"There was a whole class dedicated to it," Candice added.

Another story struck my mind as the pair entered the house, slamming the door despite my insistence not to slam the door.

Mild-Mannered Man Murders Ungrateful Teenagers.

It was really more of a headline for the front page of a newspaper than anything.

I really needed to talk with the two of them about respecting their parents. I stood there momentarily, thinking about how to handle that conversation, but it kept veering off into my fantasizing about strangling the ungrateful brats. "Who is the dork now?!"

Deciding I wasn't getting anywhere with that particular task, I turned my attention to the honey-do list my wife had prepared. I handled a few quick tasks like changing light bulbs and reminding the teenagers of their chores, for which I was called a dork again. I was heading back downstairs when I heard the four-year-old, Louise, call for me from her room.

"Daddy!" she cried.

"Yes, my sweet little angel?" I asked, popping my head into her room.

"My teapot broke," she said, holding a plastic teapot with a broken handle.

"Oh, dear. How did that happen?"

Louise proceeded to tell me a long, rambling, incoherent story that I couldn't follow. Something about Princess Panda—a stuffed panda she had forced into a frilly princess dress—having a fit over something. It made no sense to me. Pandas weren't prone to fits of anger and did not drink tea or have their own monarchy. It was completely illogical. The order of the scenes was also wrong; she started in the middle, then went back to the beginning, told me the end, then told me the beginning again, and then some nonsense in the middle. It was as if the four-year-old had no experience telling stories. That sort of storytelling shenanigans might be acceptable for a Tarantino film, but I would not stand for it.

I took Louise and her tea set down to the garage, where I applied some super glue and twine to keep it in place while the glue set.

See, that's how you tell a story—clean-cut and linear—no jumping back and forth like some hooligan or four-year-old toddler who barely recognizes the English language.

Satisfied that I was still a hero in one of my children's eyes, I sent the atrocious storyteller to the kitchen to help her mother prepare supper while I walked through the yard picking up sticks, rocks, and toys that had accumulated. As part of the local Home Owner's Association, I had a duty and obligation to maintain the length of my grass to no more than 2.5 inches. As I tried to impress upon my children and everyone who entered the Boreing Insurance Company, restrictions and rules were the only way to have fun.

Once I cleaned the yard, I pulled the old manual reel mower out of the shed. The HOA liked to keep things quiet in the neighborhood, and I have a grand old time following the rules. When we were dating, my wife and I first argued when she tried introducing "house rules" for Monopoly to make the game not take as long. I spent the next three hours insisting to her that if the game were meant to be short and enjoyable, the creators would have made different rules. Piñatas were meant to be broken, not rules, missy.

Hey, that's an idea.

Monopoly: The Novel by Ted Allen. A family sits down to play Monopoly, but the entire story is marked by shouting and arguments about following the rules to maximize the fun.

I'll never get Hasbro's licensing for that. Also, who has fights over an exhilarating game like Monopoly? No reasonable person, that's who.

"Blast my unrealistic ideas."

While mowing the lawn, I took the opportunity to throw other ideas around, mostly involving landscaping. As I snaked through the backyard, Frankie came ambling out of the house and fell over with a thump. Frankie had long since given up the pretense of lightly lowering himself to the ground. It was much easier to just pitch over to one side.

"Frankie, you have to move," I said as I passed. Then on the next pass, I repeated, "Seriously, Frankie. I need to cut the grass there."

I let Frankie rest on the cool grass for as long as possible, mowing down all other grass until only the patch he laid on remained.

"C'mon, get up," I said, tapping his behind with the toe of my shoe.

Frankie lifted his head and huffed at me before laying his head down again.

For several minutes I attempted to get Frankie to move. I pulled him, pushed him, sat on him, called him, and even tried bribing him with food. At no point did the fat mongrel move. As I stood with my hands on my hips, trying to figure out where I lost control over my life, another novel idea came to mind.

Let Sleeping Dogs Lie by Ted Allen. A divorced father must keep up appearances after the family dog dies, pretending everything is fine to avoid the wrath of his ex-wife and the tears of his children.

It's like Weekend at Bernie's but for a dead dog. People love dogs! People love stories about death!

...but people probably wouldn't want to read about a dead dog. That was a bit of a downer. Not to mention PETA would have a cow. And then shit bricks over the term having a cow.

With the sun setting in the sky, time was running out for politeness with Frankie. So I grabbed Frankie's ankles and pulled, straining and grunting as I tried getting him to move even just a few feet.

"Hey!" I heard Bryson yell out from his bedroom window. "Why are you tugging on Boner?"

"His name is Frankie," I said. "And I need to mow."

"He's trying to nap. Leave my Boner alone."

"He's not your Boner, he's my Boner!"

Candice then appeared in the window beside Bryson's.

"Why are you two shouting?" she asked.

"Dad's bothering Boner," Bryson explained.

"Leave our Boner alone! He's being cute and sleeping."

"Can we please stop shouting the word Boner?" I shouted. "The neighbors can hear us!"

"What is all this yelling about?" I heard from over the fence.

I felt my cheeks flush as I turned to see the neighbor, Jerry, peering over the fence, his face confused and annoyed.

"Our dad is trying to move our Boner," Candice said.

Jerry's face became less annoyed and much more I'm-about-to-call-the-police.

"The children call the dog, *Frankie*, Boner," I explained.

Spotting the tub of lard we call a dog, Jerry perked up. "Ohh. Can I come over to pet your Boner?"

"No, you may not pet my Boner!" I yelled, spittle flying from my mouth. "None of you may pet my Boner!"

Frustrated by the whole proceeding, I stormed into the house amid Bryson, Candice, and Jeff's childish giggles. I would simply have to get outside next time Bon—er, Frankie, got up.

Soon, it was time for the family to sit down to dinner. It was relatively uneventful, the way life is supposed to be. Bryson and Candice told as little about their day as they could get away with. Louise told a wildly unorganized story about her day, leaving out my fixing her teapot completely. Megan ran some errands with Louise—which Louise left out as well, I would add. I told them about my day and the various ideas for a new novel. I also told them my joke with Jeff about insurance policies not covering suicide. None of them got the joke. It's hard to explain insurance jokes to people who are not in the business. It's even harder to get them to sit around and listen to you explain why the joke was funny and how the insurance business worked.

After dinner, while the family watched TV, I perused the family library looking for inspiration on a new novel. But all I could ever come up with were terrible parodies of the original, with thinly veiled new names for the main characters—Schmerlock Schmolmes, the Pretty Okay Gotsby, Barry Otter, the World's First Aquatic Wizard.

The more I thought about it, the harder it became. The harder it became, the more stressed I was. The more stressed I was, the more I thought about it. It was a damned vicious cycle.

Periodically, I would pop into the living room to pitch one of the ideas to the family in desperation.

"What about a novel set on an ocean liner doomed to sink?" I said. "Could be a love story, perhaps?"

"That's called *Titanic*, you dork," Candice said.

"Oh, right. What about an everyman cop trying to reunite with his wife amidst a terrorist takeover of an office building?"

"*Die Hard*," Bryson said. "You dork."

"What about a father who tries to kill his children?" I said, sneering.

"I think that's *The Shining*, dear," Megan chimed in.

My efforts to find my next great novel remained fruitless the rest of the night. Only when the kids had been sent to bed and the wife and I were getting ready to sleep, did I give up on the idea for the night.

I lay in bed for quite some time, staring at the ceiling, frustrated and devoid of ideas. Perhaps I would have to join a writer's group of some kind; get back in touch with my fellow creatives.

That's when it hit me. The answer had been staring me in the face the entire day, and I couldn't see it. What was more personal to me than the very day I just had?

The Write Story by Ted Allen. A man struggles to find a new novel idea to revitalize his career. It was bold. It was different. It had comedic possibilities. It had a play on words in the title.

As with all the other ideas that day, however, my interest deflated when reality came crashing down one more time. It was a fine idea, but it would, at best, produce a precisely 4,180 word short story.

Besides, who would take the time to read something so ridiculous?

Estate Matters
by Shannon McKeehen

Shannon McKeehen holds an MFA in Creative Writing (Mills College) and a PhD in Composition (Kent State). Her work has appeared in Guide to Kulchur, The Toledo Free Press, *and other places. Her chapbook,* Barbra in Shadow, *is available on Amazon. Shannon grew up in central Ohio but has lived and taught in Toledo, Kent, and Akron; she currently teaches composition and technical writing at Tiffin University.*

Grief is love and
love is grief and
this house held you
until you grew
into
your grief—
and when
you are quiet,
you can hear
the floors
breathing—
with the womb
at the center,
wide and much too warm.
Love is grief and
it calluses over and
you try to just
let it
but you can't.
This house held you
until you
reluctantly
grew up and out,
arms outstretched
and aching.
Can you ever forgive me?

Lake House

by Scott Jessop

Most of the time, Scott Jessop is a corporate video and TV commercial writer, producer, and director. His work has appeared in dozens of publications, including the Saturday Evening Post, The Red Earth Review, Penduline Press, Jitter Press, Bewildering Stories, El Portal, Adelaide Literary Magazine, The Phoenix, Weber-The Contemporary West, *and Hireath Publishing's anthology,* The Martian Wave. *Scott recently published* Ruxton Springs: Dark Tales of the West, *a collection of short stories, and he was recently named a finalist for the 2023 Canopus Awards.*

The train from Berkley was late. Had it been on time, Grace would've missed Ben on the station's giant video screens. She stared at the screen hoisted ten meters above the station floor, his face in close-up. There he was, much older, shorter, and thinner than she remembered, his head bulbous from the Paget's disease that gripped him in his later years as if his great mind were trying to push out of the skull that imprisoned it.

People swirled around her in the summer heat. The A/C was not functioning in the cavern of the station. The nervous bustle of commuters who are always late and drowning in the underground, clawing toward the surface for gasps of air. As always, there was a knot in the pit of her stomach. As always, a bit of confusion mixed with ritual. Her feet clad in sneakers, Grace clutched her sensible shoes in a netted bag, and in her other hand, her portfolio, and within it, the presentation she was making to the Pacifica Economic Council. Her brain kept rehearsing answers to questions that would not come, even though she knew it was best not to anticipate.

Grace's mind raced on its own. She just happened to look up. It was a reflexive glance at the screen because she told herself she likes to be informed. These were remarkable times, after all. Six new nations, born in violence from the tattered remains of a once great empire, fell into economic ruin. And there he was, on his face, the old defiance, the fight.

When they first talked 45 years before, she remembered, he was intrigued by the child who had invaded his space. She shivered on the wet seat of Ben's rented bass boat in a western inlet of Mantanzas Lake in Central Illinois, back when it was still called Illinois, as the first red rays of early September daylight glittered through the trees. She remembered the water flat and mirrored, dark at the edges with streaks of red as they waited in a cove opposite the lake house for the fish to start biting. This was bass fishing, Ben told her, his thin blond hair lying flat on his head, heavy breaths through his nose as he centered himself in the moment. Only eleven and city-bred, Grace had no idea what was happening. What was this sitting in a boat with poles and lines? She thought about her warm bed at the rented house and almost cried. Adults held no interest in her, or they had no more interest than her classmates. She just wanted to dig for bits of junk in the muddy sand near the shore, swim in the dark waters, or be alone with the many thoughts invading her vacation.

The shallows were best, he said, when they crossed the lake, and then he fell quiet and sipped coffee from the plastic cup on the Thermos. They sat silently in the boat for over half an hour before Ben leaned over.

"I like the jigs," he whispered, removing a fuzzy thing from the tackle box he bought at Walmart the previous afternoon. In the few days she had known him, this time in the boat was their longest conversation. "Bass are opportunistic hunters. They go after wounded prey."

"Like lions on the Serengeti, they hunt the wounded gazelle," Grace spewed loudly. "It's called conservation of energy. They may not get another meal for days, so they want to expel as little energy as possible. The gazelles know this, which is why they run from the wounded member of the herd."

The words flowed out like a spigot, blasting useless information. He shushed the girl, thought better of it, and said, "You got it. That's exactly right. Like lions, but we need to be quiet to trap our prey." His sad, blue eyes—gray and distant the day before like a person drained of character and blood—were now bright and lively. The sport brought life back to his cheeks. Taking a pair of needle-nosed pliers, Ben crimped one of the links between the shiny, silver plates so that the lure would move with a hitch. He tied it to the line on Grace's pole, squinting at the lower third of his progressive lensed glasses with his lips pulled tight and his fat fingers working the knot. "Do you know how to cast?"

She shook her head no.

He turned the pole over and pointed to the reel. "This is the spool, and this is the release. The dial sets the tension. This is the brake. I've set it on high since you're new. And this is the crank." He turned it to show her how it worked.

He hooked his finger under the line on his pole and drew a few inches. He pulled his arm back. "Look where you want to cast and snap your wrist." His cast smoothly played out to the reeds near the shore. He reeled back in and handed it to her.

She took her pole and snapped her wrist in the motion he showed her, but the lure only fell inches from the end of the pole.

"That's my fault," he said, taking the pole in his hands. "Press the release before you cast, then let it go as you snap your wrist. Press it again just as it hits the water, so your line won't tangle. It takes some practice to get the timing right."

He motioned for her to try again. She did with similar results and tossed the pole down in frustration. Most things came easy for Grace, and for those that did not, she quickly abandoned them. In this way, she seemed to excel, avoiding the failures of her classmates. Ben was not as easily fooled. He placed the pole in her hand and told her to cast again.

"This is stupid," she said, tossing the pole into the well of the boat. Ben sighed and cast his line in the opposite direction.

She poked at the gear lying in a fetid pool of water at the bottom of the boat with her toe. They sat in silence, watching the Black Crappies occasionally breaking the surface to snatch breakfast.

Bored, she pointed to the lake, "This used to be the river. Then two hundred years ago, there was an earthquake, the New Madrid earthquake in Missouri, the most powerful earthquake in recorded history. It rang church bells in Boston and shifted the river's course to the west, leaving this lake. That's why it's so long and narrow. The only thing separating the lake from the river is that little bank. Every few years, the river floods, and it replenishes the lake. That's why there are always fish in here."

"What grade are you in?" he asked. "Sixth?"

She pulled her jacket close and turned her head to the sun. "I'm supposed to be, but I'll be going into eighth grade this year."

"Wow."

"They call it gifted and talented." To this, he snickered, and it embarrassed Grace. She dropped her head and shut up.

The current pulled the boat into the lake as Ben sipped his coffee and gave his pole the occasional pull. The sun was higher. Some distant prairie thunderstorms pushed a warm wind across the plains to ripple the water. The heron left their treetop nests for the Illinois sky. Across the lake, Grace's mother swallowed her morning Scotch on the deck of the lake house while her Aunt Miriam was on the upper deck sipping coffee and sneaking a cigarette. Soon her mother would go to the kitchen to make one of her vegan breakfasts that Ben would pretend to enjoy, and then he'd make an excuse to go into town, where he would plant himself in front of a plate of biscuits and sausage gravy and a couple of eggs.

Lydia, Grace's mother, started taking her to Airbnbs the spring the pandemic hit and after her divorce was finalized. They were nice respites from their dreary bungalow near the Bradley campus, where Lydia worked as her father and mother did before her. None of her family attended the school but worked on the grounds, maintained the heating plant, and answered phones in the bursar's office. With fantastic dreams and little ambition, Lydia went through life at a steady level, low to the ground and beneath fate's radar.

It was Miriam's idea to share the lake house. She said they could all use a break, and the lake was a nice contrast from the desert where she lived with Ben.

When Lydia and Grace arrived, Miriam and Ben were already there and claimed the bedroom overlooking the lake. Lydia got straight to work hauling in groceries while Grace hugged Miriam and told her how much she loved her. Grace was a sweetheart in that way. "I'm so glad to see you," she said with her arms wrapped around Miriam. Ben was on the deck, sunglasses on, debating whether he should help. If he did, someone would scold him for not thinking them capable, and if he didn't, he'd be seen as rude, or so went the quiet deliberation in his head.

Lydia separated Grace from Miriam, "Go. Go outside," she said, seeing Ben on the deck. She frowned, started to say something to Miriam, stopped, and started wiping down the kitchen counters with a sponge she rinsed out in the sink. "How's Oklahoma?"

"We're living in New Mexico now," said Miriam. "It's so much better for my art, and Ben is teaching at a community college."

"Oh, you mean he got a job?"

Miriam feigned offense, "He's a college economics professor," she protested with her hand well-placed over her heart.

Lydia waved the air. "Oh, it was something Gram said. You know how she gets."

"Well, I'm not. Not really," said Ben standing at the door holding an empty glass. "I work at a curio shop in the Plaza for thirteen an hour, and I teach two basic economics courses at the community college. Your mom is right, Miriam. I'm unemployable."

"I mean, you have had a lot of jobs," Lydia said, putting groceries away to avoid looking at Miriam or Ben. "Illinois State, Colorado State, Texas, that little college in Oklahoma, and now you say a community college in New Mexico, it's, you know, um..."

"Well," said Ben crossing to the sink to deposit the glass and opening the Fridge for a bottle of iced tea. "I'm a dangerous man."

"Don't be so catastrophic," said Miriam. His damaged ego always needed the bulwarks propped up, and Miriam took on this task despite telling herself she was not his fixer. She encouraged him to find new opportunities, praised him for finding a job at the shop, and thanked him for doing chores around the house. Without it, he would sit in the muck of his unraveling life, pining for the days before the theory seized him and he published it. Few in his field embraced it. Others condemned it as nonsense, while most were alarmed. It was too controversial of a theory and too early for an unknown professor without tenure. Still, he was single-minded in those days and gripped in the self-deluded belief that it would be embraced, as it should've been, as deliverance and him a savior.

Miriam, having dumped or been dumped by her previous beau, decided to take a few art classes at Illinois State. She drove to Normal and enrolled. There was the popular economics professor older than other adjunct professors, handsome in a nerdy way, with his groupies following him around as if tied on a leash he held. She met him at an off-campus coffee shop when he ordered a zucchini muffin, and the clerk pointed to her, saying she had just bought the last one. Miriam offered to split it. They spent the next several hours staring into each other's eyes in deep conversation punctuated by stupid dad jokes until they both ran off to class. They fell into bed later that evening.

Ben returned to the deck at the back of the house. Grace had taken his position on the chaise longue and had one of his books in her hands. She was tiny for her age, skinny with big tufts of unbrushed tangles of brown hair and oversized sunglasses. Ben noticed Grace was reading and not just looking at the book, a collection of poems well beyond her years. Her head swayed back and forth across the page, and her lower lip slid in and out as she moved through the stanzas.

Water lapped the shore below; Ben's eyes followed the ripples left from a passing speedboat to the green line of forest dotted with white herons resting in the trees on the other shore half a mile away.

A boat with several men and their fishing gear went by. Ben's father had a pontoon boat. His Pride plied the waters of Lake McConaughey in western Nebraska and Cherry Creek Reservoir in south Denver whenever he and his father could get away with a pole and a tackle box. In those days, Ben worked construction with his dad and fished on the weekends. Fly fishing on the South Platte near Tappan Mountain. Walleye in Michigan. Once deep-sea fishing in the Gulf of Mexico to fulfill his Hemingway dreams. He enjoyed the challenge, the duality of focus on the task, and the peace with his thoughts. On a fishing trip to Alabama, he met an English professor from Auburn. During their brief weekend affair, he encouraged Ben to go to college. Economics was hardly his first choice, but Ben was drawn to math as fishing drew him.

He could hear Miriam in the kitchen, "He's not just my friend."

Then Lydia said, "Well, boyfriend."

"Life partner. We've been together five years now."

And Lydia, "Yeah, five years, and how many houses?"

Ben stared at the little girl, pulled another chair, and sat down. Picking up a collection of T.S. Eliot, he handed it to Grace and took the copy of Bukowski's Sampler from her. She took little notice, and he treated her with the same detached demeanor he had for most people. To Grace, Miriam's boyfriend seemed different, and she liked that. Grace preferred existing in her world since few could relate to her. Ben sat beside her, read, scribbled on a legal pad, circled lines of poetry, and stared across the water.

"Oh hey," she said, finally.

He looked at her and smiled but said nothing in return. She got up.

"You want anything?" she asked.

He shook his head and pointed to his Snapple. He continued reading, jotting down notes from time to time, and played with a curious boney knot on the back of his skull, dismissing it as nothing but feeling it and wondering when it formed. Lately, it has been much the same with people. He ignored them but kept them close. He was rarely engaging. Grace returned with a bottle of water and some bizarre Japanese vegan snack and sat beside him. She picked up the book of poems, started reading, and that was how they spent their afternoon.

Yesterday, he docked the bass boat below the house and invited Grace to go fishing.

Today, he had a strike. The pole went from level to bending to the water, and Ben steadied his feet for the fight. He reeled in and leaned back, then eased forward, then back again. The bass broke the surface and twisted its head, trying to free itself from the hooks in the lure. Ben leaned hard. "Grab the net," he said as he reeled it closer to the boat.

She froze, watching the bass jump out of the water.

"Gracie, the net." No one called her Gracie. She grabbed the net and then looked at him. What was she supposed to do now?

He was laughing and shouting. "Whoa!" He turned to Grace. "See how I pull him in, forcing him to work hard to try to escape? Then I relax a little letting him think he's won, but before he can rest, I pull back again and reel fast." He leaned hard and reeled in. "Now, when he gets close to the boat, you swoop down with the net and pull him out of the water."

"Me?" She was shaking.

"You can do it, Gracie," he said between breaths.

"I don't know how," she whined.

"Smart kid like you? You'll figure it out," he said with a wink.

The fish was near the edge of the boat. Thrashing. Twisting, but less than before. Ben reeled in, and as the fish's head slipped out of the water, Grace moved in with the net and scooped it up. The fish knew it was doomed and went limp. Ben grabbed it by the chin, his thumb in its mouth, and lifted it. The big fish gasping for air made Grace sad, but Ben seemed pleased.

He reached into its mouth, pulled the hook, and inspected its gills. "Tough guy," he said, then he tossed it back into the water and let it go, which thrilled Grace. "First fish I've caught in almost ten years," he said.

That evening Lydia lit a fire in the pit near the shore. Grace and Lydia roasted marshmallows while Ben and Miriam sipped their beer and spoke in low voices. "Realistically, you haven't tried that many places," Miriam told Ben. "You just have to find the right fit."

She was good at platitudes, just not applying them, and Ben sat in silence, staring at the fire. He wanted to tell her that for all their talk of academic freedom, colleges depended on funding from the state or donors, and those monied voices demanded his head, or better, his capitulation in exchange for their support. That it wasn't a matter of trying, he was trying, but unspoken in the feedback from the places he was reaching out to was that he needed to let the book and the theory go. Not completely repudiate his work; that would be a disaster, but let it slip away. Her intentions were good, but she saw the problem differently than he did. She saw a job to be won, and he saw the political nature of his labors. It was arrogance, he knew, to hold fast to what had ruined him. It was as if he woke up in an alternate reality where he spoke a language no one understood, and she advocated that he be an orator.

"If you just," she started.

"Applied 'myself?'" he finished.

"We're doing fine. You can always go back to construction work."

"I'm like the fish Gracie and I caught today. I'm hooked in the mouth, and the more I resist, the more exhausted I become."

"Stop resisting. Let it go."

"I wonder how many fish think that way," he said.

They left the fire, walked down the shore past the kayaks, and sat on a log. Miriam was packing a bowl. Lydia insisted they smoke cannabis away from Grace. "Jesus. You know this comes from a place of privilege," said Miriam. "Everything you've ever wanted was easy for you: school, work, position. You've written this theory, and the entrenched powers and rich corporations want your head. For the first time in your life, you've been challenged."

"What am I supposed to do, Miriam?" he asked. "I'm selling trinkets to tourists."

"Change is the dark force of the universe, and it's coming whether you like it or not. What was it you said, 'We need to be comfortable with being uncomfortable.' Well, buddy, here's your chance." She passed the pipe and the lighter to him, part of the weed etiquette that gives the person who did not pack the bowl the initial flame when the cannabis is fresh, uncharred, and the THC crystals are untainted for the maximum effect. He nodded, lit the weed, and inhaled.

The following day, Ben and Grace fished, and, in the afternoon, he returned to his pile of books, Bukowski, Hart Crane, and the like. All subversive poets, but as he would say, all poets are subversive. Then after a moment of hesitation, he turned to the economic notes he took while composing his theory. He thumbed them the way a widower goes through photos. After dinner, he grabbed his old laptop, fired it up, and wrote for hours. His fingers pounded the keys. It could be heard throughout the house. Though he was too young to have ever spent much time at a manual typewriter, he wrote like he was on one. Bang. Bang. Bangity-bang. And after midnight, when he was done, he went to bed without saying a word.

At 4:30 AM, he woke Grace, and they were back on the water.

With the lure tied and ready, she tried to cast again. This time it flew a few yards, and Ben nodded. He showed her how to reel it in to keep the lure moving slowly, and when it reached the boat, she cast again. This time the line flew ten yards. They waited.

The current moved the lure, and she pulled on the line from time to time. The line jerked hard as the sun shattered the horizon, turning the red sky blue.

She turned the reel handle as she had seen Ben do, fast then slower. "Good, good," he said. "Now, crank and pull." She did as he said, alternating between pulling and reeling until the bass jumped out of the water. It pulled her nearly out of the boat. Ben laughed, "That's a big one. Nearly five pounds." He grabbed the net.

She fought the big fish for several minutes until she got it close to the boat. Ben scooped it up in the net. He showed her how to hold it, and she pinched its chin as he took a picture. Then he removed the hook and lowered the fish back into the water.

"Live to fight another day, big guy," he said.

"Why'd you do that?" Grace asked.

Ben smiled. "I fish for the sport. Besides, do you think your mom would let us cook and eat it?"

Grace laughed, and they sat back down.

"Fishing teaches you to be patient," said Ben, "and then work like hell when the time is right."

"And what does the fish learn?" Gracie asked.

Ben laughed and poured himself a coffee. "I'm not sure, I'm not a fish, but I let them go because they're worth more in the water. Let him spawn and flourish, and there will be more like him. And now, you've got a story to tell," he said with a wink.

She looked at him, then down to the boat, and said, "Everyone says I talk too much."

"Why is that?"

"Because I do."

He laughed. "I mean, why do you suppose you talk so much."

Grace looked out over the water, hoping to see the free fish break the surface. Lost for a bit in the adventure of the moment. "I suppose it's because I just think stuff is cool."

He smiled, "Me too. Do you think you're smart?"

"Teachers tell me I am."

Ben nodded. "But…"

"Some of my friends play basketball; others play instruments. Mom knows how to cook. Miriam knows how to make cool jewelry. I know stuff," she said without looking at him. No one had asked her this before, and kids clam up when asked prickly questions. Grace opened. "They know stuff. I know stuff. What's the big deal?"

Ben tossed the last of his coffee into the lake. "That's a trait I've noticed with the smartest people I know. They assume everyone is smart. It's just the information you know, and you want to share it. And sometimes you find something or see something that no one else has seen, and you think they'll be as excited about it as you are, but often they're not." He trailed off briefly and then lowered the motor into the water. "We should be getting back. Look, your aunt is waving at us."

Miriam stood next to her niece in her peasant skirt and halter top, fashionably out of time and straining to see what they were doing across the lake. "My mom says you can't hold a job," Grace said.

He had tried for years to be accepted by Miriam's family, but they always considered him an outsider, and this week was set up by her to get him closer to them. It was a difficult thing for him to do. His natural detachment and nagging depression set him apart from their often-boisterous family. Still, Miriam's mother didn't like him and wasn't shy about letting the family or him know it. She wanted Miriam to get back with her urologist ex-husband.

"'I should've been a pair of ragged claws scuttling across the floors of a silent sea,'" he said.

Grace looked at him, "What does that mean?"

"Nothing."

"I heard you tell Mom you were a dangerous man. Did you hurt somebody?" Grace asked.

"No." He set their poles down and uselessly moved the tackle box as if stowed in this magical spot, the boat would fly across the water, but it was something to do to occupy his eyes.

"Then what?"

"Ideas can be dangerous, Gracie." He turned the motor over and let it idle. "Do you know what economics is?" She shook her head. "It's the study of making things, distributing things, and buying things. That's what I do, and I believe that society's greatest asset isn't oil, timber, or arable land. It isn't their capital. It's their people."

"That doesn't sound dangerous," Grace said. "Sounds like a big duh."

Ben smiled. "Great. A kid gets it. But that idea scares people, especially those invested in the status quo—how things are. So, I learned to shut up. To keep it to myself. That was a mistake."

They sailed across the lake. Lydia had cooked various grains and a fruit compote for breakfast. After breakfast, Grace went with Ben to return the bass boat to the marina, and they drove into town and grabbed a cheeseburger and a chocolate malt.

"I'm glad you're my uncle," Grace said between bites of French fries. "Even though you're not my real uncle, just my aunt's boyfriend."

"Uncle Ben? Heaven's no," he said. "Call me Ben. You know, like we're friends. Because we're friends."

She smiled and took a bite. "Are you and Aunt Miriam going back to New Mexico?"

"Yeah."

"And you're going to work in the gift shop?"

"It's a means to an end, Gracie. No one can stop me from publishing. Especially when I'm the publisher," he said, taking a smug bite from his burger. "Keep fighting to the end. Maybe, that's what the fish learns."

"Well," she said, "that's what they get for throwing you back in." He laughed and gave her a high-five.

They parted later that day. Ben and Miriam drove back to Albuquerque, where he got straight to work. He started his press, built a Utopian business in the desert, and created wealth for himself and his associates amid the capitalist decline.

*****

By the time Grace reached high school a few years later, she had learned that the paper Ben had written at the lake house was a series of predictions of the coming collapse and ways to mitigate the effects. As his work proved prescient, he was offered and accepted a position at Stanford. Grace went to the University of Chicago. She wrote to him weekly, knowing his emails were being read. He and Miriam could not make it to Chicago for her graduation because of the war.

During the collapse, Ben's ideas reminded many of Trotsky and led to the charges that he was a communist when he was more Christ-like in his revolution—angry, thoughtful, and resigned to the eventual sacrifice if only to prove himself.

On the video screen at the Pacifica Capital Station in the Presidio, the news showed Ben flanked by two Alabaster Guards of the Republic of Deseret. He had gone there several years before at 88 when he should've been retired, driven to help the nascent nation rebuild its economy. "Convicted of Heresy," it said on the screen. They had beaten him, starved him. An unkempt beard lay in patches across his gaunt face, but he wore contumaciousness like a bespoke suit. His defiance was defiant even in defeat. "Sentenced to death."

On that last day at the lake, Ben had snagged a big bass before they returned the boat. It struck his line with enough force that the pole nearly broke from his hands. He reeled and leaned, reeled and leaned until the great fish broke the water. It twisted and turned in the air, dove back into the deep water, and pulled on the line, jerking in one direction and then the opposite.

"Jesus, it's headed back at us," said Ben with a click of his teeth.

Grace grabbed the net, but the fish went under the boat dragging the line with it and pulling Ben off his feet. The pole bent over in a great arc until the line snapped, sending Ben's pole tumbling across the boat.

In a final insult, they saw the fish's tail sweep the water before it disappeared in the safety of the reeds.

The TV screen went to the next story. Grace lowered her head, gathered her collection of Ben's formulas and theories with her spin added to them, and walked to the stairs, confident in the lessons he had taught her on the calm waters of Matanzas Lake.

Fight.